The Last Words of Dutch Schultz
of Dutch Schultz

Also by William S. Burroughs

Exterminator!
Junkie
Naked Lunch
Nova Express
The Soft Machine
The Ticket That Exploded
The Wild Boys
Yage Letters (with Allen Ginsberg)

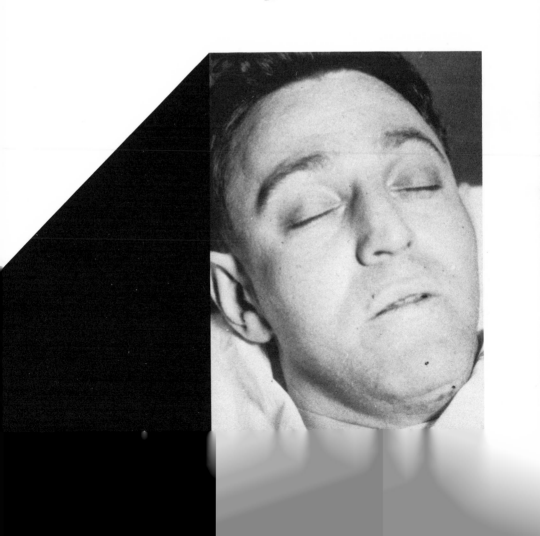

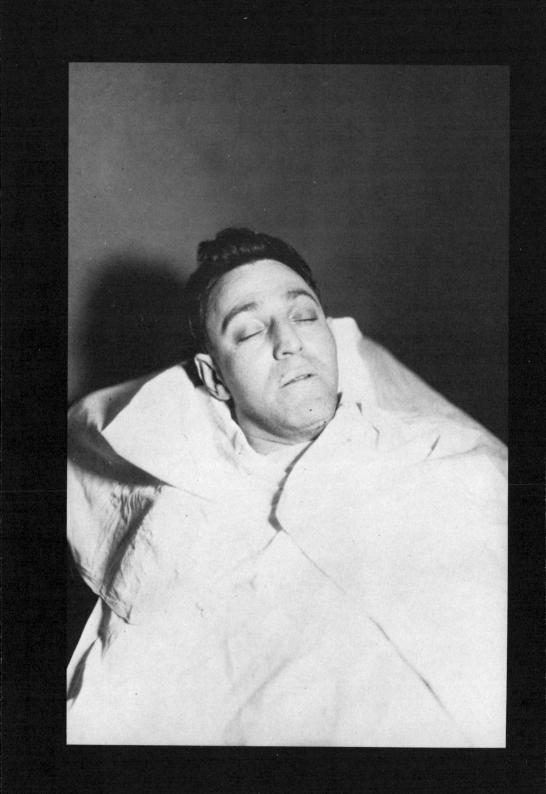

William S. Burroughs
The Last Words of Dutch Schultz
A Fiction in the Form of a Film Script

Don G.D

A RICHARD SEAVER BOOK

THE VIKING PRESS

NEW YORK

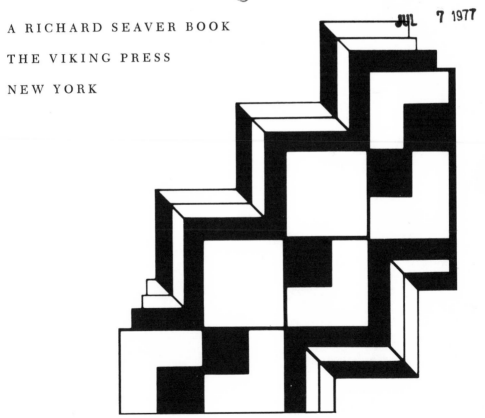

Photo Credits: Pages iii, iv, viii, 1, 5, 73, 76, 106, 108, 111:
David Budd; pages 2, 71: Mayotte Magnus; pages 17, 18, 21,
34, 41, 69, 82, 88, 90, 98, 100, 107, 113: Wide World Photos;
page 37: Culver Pictures; p. 43: Alain Resnais; page 61:
Schomberg Collection, NYPL. All other photographs courtesy
the author and David Budd. Reprinted with permission.

To David Budd

The Last Words of Dutch Schultz

1

INTERIOR. HOSPITAL ROOM. DAWN. MEDIUM SHOT.

Two detectives and a police stenographer sit in straight-backed chairs, facing camera. They are arranged in a rough semicircle, the two detectives facing the head of the bed, the stenographer sitting with his ear to the head of the bed. Neither the bed nor Dutch are visible in this take, which is shot from where the bed would be. Expressions of boredom, frustration, weariness on the faces of the two detectives. The detectives are played by the same actors who will later appear as Abe Landau and Lulu Rosencrantz. The police stenographer—thin, grey, spectral, behind steel-rimmed glasses—sits expressionless, pencil poised over his clipboard. Over a period of 24 hours Dutch spoke about 2,000 words. Obviously there were long periods when he did not say anything. This shot of the two detectives and the stenographer is shown in slow motion, which is not readily apparent owing to the immobility of the actors.

HOSPITAL SOUND EFFECTS
(These are actual hospital recordings made over a period of time and edited for most striking and bizarre effects. This edited hospital soundtrack is repeated in various combinations throughout this and other hospital scenes.) The entire transcript of Dutch's last words . . . about 2,000 words . . . will be recorded on hospital location. Most of this recording will of course be in the voice of Dutch, but other actors who figure in his delirium will speak some of the lines. Dutch's mother, Albert Stern, Jules Martin, George Weinberg, Frances Schultz . . . This recording will be used as background sound effects at intervals throughout the film, as indicated in script.

Police stenographer starts to write this down.
Cut-in flash of boys running and beckoning from playgrounds and bridges.
A skull-faced porter turns around: the number on his cap is 23.

Voice of Dutch off-screen:
A boy has never wept . . .

. . . or dashed a thousand Kim.

LONG PAUSE

Flash of picket fence and lilac bed. Cut back to hospital room. The police stenographer stops writing. The detectives lean forward.

In the voice of Albert Stern:
Did you hear me?

1st Detective:
Who shot you?

3

2

INTERIOR. HALL. NIGHT. CLOSE-UP.

Old-fashioned door with scroll work. The door opens. Doctor Stern—thin, tubercular, sad—stands in the doorway.

CRY OF NEW-BORN BABY

Doctor Stern:
You can come in now, Mr Flegenheimer. A fine boy. Where can I wash my hands?

Close-up of Mr Flegenheimer standing in the hall. He is a heavy man with a mustache and watch chain. There is a glint of absent restlessness in his eye. Not quite the proud father.

Mr Flegenheimer:
First door on the left, Doctor.

As Mr Flegenheimer points to the bathroom door, the word MEN appears and the door changes to green door of a men's room in a bar.

SOUND OF RUNNING WATER

3

INTERIOR. WASHROOM OF PALACE CHOP HOUSE. NIGHT. MEDIUM SHOT.

Dutch with his back to the camera is washing his hands. His face in mirror. Seen in the mirror the door opens behind him. Standing in the doorway is a composite figure of Albert Stern, Charlie Workman, Lulu Rosencrantz, with pistol leveled. Six-frame take.

Voice of Dutch Schultz off-screen (puzzled and hesitant):
I don't know sir. I don't even know who was with me. I was in the toilet, and when I reached the . . . the boy came at me.

Figure fires from doorway seen in mirror. Dutch grabs his back with right hand and twists to the floor looking at blood on his hands.

PISTOL SHOT

FUSILLADE OF SHOTS OFF-SCREEN
HOSPITAL SOUND EFFECTS
LAST WORD RECORDINGS

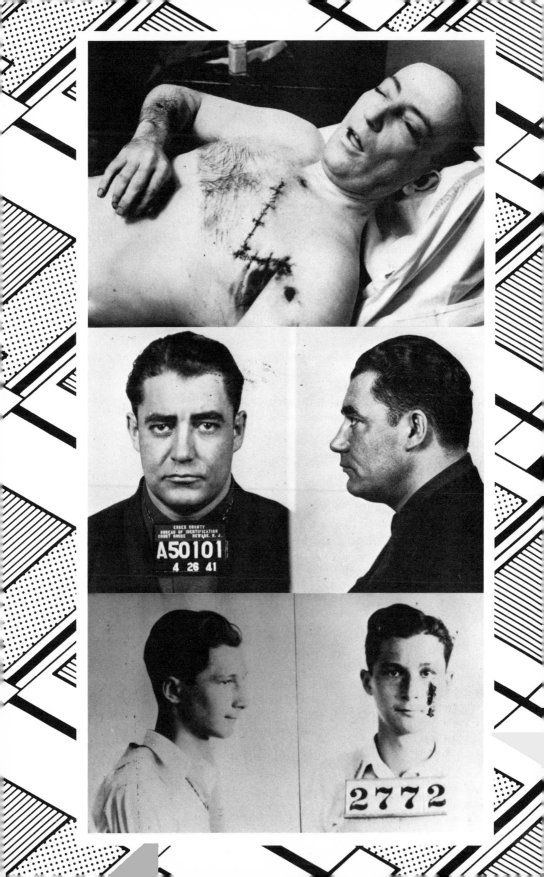

2772

ACTION | SOUND

4

INTERIOR. BACK ROOM OF PALACE CHOP HOUSE. NIGHT. MEDIUM SHOT.

Camera in doorway. Broken beer glasses, bloody account sheets, an adding machine, a smoking cigar with chewed end, three men sprawled on the floor. Abe Landau heaves himself off the floor and staggers to the doorway, a .45 in his right hand. He supports himself against doorjamb.

UNHURRIED FOOTSTEPS GOING AWAY OFF-SCREEN

5

INTERIOR. BAR OF THE PALACE CHOP HOUSE. NIGHT. TRACKING SHOT.

Facing the camera, Abe Landau pulls himself along the bar rail with his left hand. His great paunch is ripped by slugs but he is still obstinate as a dying snake.

6

INTERIOR. WASHROOM OF PALACE CHOP HOUSE. NIGHT. CLOSE-UP.

Dutch crawling toward the door.

GROANS AND HEAVY BREATHING

7

EXTERIOR. FRONT OF PALACE CHOP HOUSE. NIGHT. LONG SHOT.

Abe Landau staggers out the door. Camera pans to black car going away. Camera pans back to Abe Landau who fires one shot after the car. Screen goes dark as he collapses.

STREET SOUND OF 1935 NEW YORK

PISTOL SHOT

8
EXTERIOR. FRONT OF FLEGENHEIMER SALOON AND LIVERY STABLE. DAWN. LONG SHOT.

FROGS, CRICKETS, BIRDS, THE NEIGH OF HORSES

9
EXTERIOR. DOORWAY OF THE SALOON. DAWN. MEDIUM SHOT.

Mr Flegenheimer and Doctor Stern shake hands. Mr Flegenheimer offers the doctor a cigar. The doctor pats his chest sadly and shakes his head. He gets into horse-drawn buggy and rides away.

SAME SOUND EFFECTS CONTINUE

10
EXTERIOR. STREET AND BUGGY GOING AWAY. DAWN. LONG SHOT.

Silver lead in the dawn sky: AUGUST 6 turns red in the rising sun. Atomic explosion on screen.
Red mushroom of the explosion becomes the rising sun. 1902 in rose letters.

LONG RUMBLING SOUND

ACTION | SOUND

11
INTERIOR. ROOM WITH ROSE WALLPAPER. SUNRISE. MEDIUM SHOT.

Red-haired boy and Mexican girl: sex scene on brass bed. This take is seven seconds repeated several times on loop, during the following takes of 1902.

12
EXTERIOR. STREET. DAY. LONG SHOT.

Horse-drawn beer trucks unloading.

13
INTERIOR. SALOON. DAY. MEDIUM SHOT.

Heavy calm bartender in striped shirt and sleeve garters hums "Sweet Sixteen" as he sets out free lunch on the bar. Behind him is a large picture titled "Custer's Last Stand." He is setting out pigs' feet, hams, corned beef, pickles, cheese, bread, sides of rare beef.

14
INTERIOR. ROOM WITH ROSE WALLPAPER. DAY. MEDIUM SHOT.

Sex scene repeats.

15
INTERIOR. SHABBY ROOM. CURTAINS DRAWN. DAY. MEDIUM SHOT.

Young man on bed in dirty underwear shorts. He is addict we will see later in the prison scene. A litter of bottles, syringes, needles, spoons, and medicine glasses on the night table. He rummages through the bottles. They are all empty. He dresses hastily.

16

EXTERIOR. STREET. DAY. LONG SHOT.

Addict steps from dark doorway into morning street. The light hurts his eyes, and he puts up a protective hand.
Sex scene projected . . . the boy's red back and buttocks on red brick houses . . . nipples, rose wallpaper, red hair on red jars in drugstore window.

17

EXTERIOR. DRUGSTORE FRONT. DAY. MEDIUM SHOT.

Group of addicts in front of drugstore. The door is opened by a white-haired druggist. The addicts troop in.

18

INTERIOR. DRUGSTORE. DAY. MEDIUM SHOT.

The druggist fills orders for cocaine, heroin, and morphine. Old Irish biddy comes in.

Druggist:
Good morning, Mrs Murphy. And what can I do for you?

Mrs Murphy (coughing):
Tincture of opium, Mr Masserang.

Druggist:
The large family size?

Mrs Murphy:
The large family size.

19
EXTERIOR. STREET. DAY. MEDIUM SHOT.

Mrs Murphy's Rooming House and Flegenheimer Saloon seen from child's eye level.
Seen over picket fence: Mrs Murphy watering her lilacs.

STREET SOUNDS

20
EXTERIOR. FLEGENHEIMER SALOON. DAY. TRACKING SHOT.

Camera tracks at child's eye level through door of saloon into saloon. A crumpled dollar falls to the floor. A child's hand reaches out and grabs it.

SALOON SOUND EFFECTS, HOSPITAL SOUND EFFECTS, LAST WORD RECORD-INGS USED IN THIS AND THE FOLLOW-ING SCENE, MIXED WITH CONVERSA-TION, ETC.

21
INTERIOR. FLEGENHEIMER SALOON. DAY. MEDIUM SHOT.

Mrs Flegenheimer pries the dollar out of young Arthur's hand and passes it back to the drunken owner.

Arthur looks at her sullenly. Now his father is standing over him, seen from the child's eyes.

Dutch looks at him, sensing the false-ness. Mr Flegenheimer is uncomfort-able under the child's gaze.

Mrs Flegenheimer:
Stop it Arthur . . . Stop it . . .
Be careful with it. I am careful my-self.

Mr Flegenheimer:
Well I see you have an eye for the dollar, young man.

22
INTERIOR. PENN STATION. DAY. MEDIUM SHOT.

Mr Flegenheimer at the ticket window. He puts his bag down.

TRAIN STATION SOUND EFFECTS

Mr Flegenheimer:
One way to St. Louis.

23

INTERIOR. FLEGENHEIMER SALOON NOW EMPTY. DAY. MEDIUM SHOT.

The furniture is gone. Arthur and Mrs Flegenheimer walk through with suitcases and bundles, aided by Mrs Murphy.

24

EXTERIOR. FRONT OF FLEGENHEIMER SALOON. DAY. MEDIUM SHOT.

The empty saloon has a façade look, like a film set. A horse-drawn moving van is in front of the door.

Driver:
Want to sit up here with me, young man?

Dutch is lifted up to the driver's seat. Mr Flegenheimer gets in with the furniture. Van moves away down the street.

25

EXTERIOR. PUBLIC SCHOOL NO. 12. DAY. LONG SHOT.

Grimy, grey, depressing.

26

INTERIOR. CLASSROOM. DAY. MEDIUM SHOT.

Albert Stern, as the teacher, is calling the roll. The blackboard behind him is covered with figures.

Teacher:
Arthur Flegenheimer . . .

27

INTERIOR. PUBLIC SCHOOL NO. 12. DAY. TRACKING SHOT.

Camera tracks through corridors, washrooms, dining halls, classrooms

SCHOOL SOUND EFFECTS

crowded with boys and girls.

Teacher's Voice (echoing through the empty school):
Arthur Flegenheimer . . . . Arthur Flegenheimer . . . Arthur Flegenheimer . . .

28
INTERIOR. CLASSROOM. DAY. CLOSE-UP.

Teacher writes "Absent" by Arthur Flegenheimer's name.

29
EXTERIOR. STREET CORNER. DAY. MEDIUM SHOT.

Dutch in street crap game. Lightning calculations, money under shoes, bets acknowledged with a barely perceptible nod. (Actual street game must be photographed and recorded for this scene.)

PLAYERS:
Five to two he eights before he sixes, etc.

30
INTERIOR. CLASSROOM. DAY. MEDIUM SHOT.

Teacher is calling on pupils to recite the multiplication table.

CRACKED VOICES INTONE MULTIPLICATION TABLE, WITH MANY ERRORS

31
EXTERIOR. STREET CORNER. DAY. MEDIUM SHOT.

Cut back to street crap game.

ACTION	SOUND

32
INTERIOR. ROOM. NIGHT. CLOSE-UP.

Mrs Flegenheimer holds up watch
and chain.

Mrs Flegenheimer:
Where did you get this, Arthur?

33
INTERIOR. CLASSROOM. DAY. MEDIUM SHOT.

Teacher calling the roll.

Teacher:
Arthur Flegenheimer . . .

34
INTERIOR. PENN STATION. DAY. LONG SHOT.

Station, passengers, porters.

TRAIN STATION SOUND EFFECTS. VOICE
OF THE TEACHER ECHOES THROUGH THE
STATION . . . "ARTHUR FLEGENHEIMER
. . . ARTHUR FLEGENHEIMER . . ."
HOSPITAL AND LAST WORDS SOUND
EFFECTS

35
INTERIOR. PENN STATION. DAY. MEDIUM SHOT.

Dutch pretends to read *The Times,*
watching man with suitcase approach ticket window. He sets suitcase down and buys ticket. When
he turns from window, Dutch and
the suitcase are gone.

36
INTERIOR. CLASSROOM. DAY. CLOSE-UP.

Teacher writes "Absent" by Arthur
Flegenheimer's name.

37
INTERIOR. COURTROOM. DAY. MEDIUM SHOT.

Dutch stands up. The judge is leaf-
ing through a file.

Bailiff:
Arthur Flegenheimer.

38
INTERIOR. COURTROOM. DAY. CLOSE-UP.

Word "truancy" in file.

Teacher's Voice:
Arthur   Flegenheimer . . . Arthur
Flegenheimer . . . Arthur   Flegen-
heimer . . .

"Petty larceny" in file.

39
EXTERIOR. STREET. DAY. MEDIUM SHOT.

Dutch snatches parcel from delivery
wagon. As he rounds corner a cop
grabs him. The parcel flies from his
hand and breaks open. It contains
a doll.

40
INTERIOR. COURTROOM. DAY. CLOSE-UP.

"Loitering with intent" in file.

41
EXTERIOR. STREET. NIGHT. MEDIUM SHOT.

Dutch and two hard-faced corner
boys in doorway watching a drunk
draped around a lamppost.

42
INTERIOR. COURTROOM. DAY. CLOSE-UP.

"Aggravated assault" in file.

43
EXTERIOR. STREET CORNER. DAY. MEDIUM SHOT.

Street crap game. A player stops the dice a split second too soon.

He is squatting down. Dutch stands over him.

Player:
They're my dice.

Dutch:
How much did you have in the pot?

Player:
Nothing.

Dutch kicks him in the mouth knocking out his front teeth.

44
INTERIOR. COURTROOM. DAY. CLOSE-UP.

"Possession of burglar tools" in file.

45
INTERIOR. PRECINCT. DAY. CLOSE-UP.

A jimmy clanks down on the desk.

46
INTERIOR. COURTROOM. DAY. MEDIUM SHOT.

A bailiff touches Dutch's arm.

Judge:
Sentenced to a year in the city detention center at Blackwell Island.

47

INTERIOR. CELL. DAY. MEDIUM SHOT.

Guard opens cell door. Two lower bunks with pillows are occupied by a tattooed Swede and a hard-eyed Sicilian. Second tier by two junkies, one old one young. Top tier on one side is anonymous middle-aged man who reads continually. Other side is empty. The Swede and the Sicilian look at Dutch in silence. Old junkie slides to the floor and walks to cell door.

Old Junkie:
How much time you bringing with you, kid?

Dutch:
A year.

Old Junkie (walking to cell door):
You can do that standing on your head. Here comes the man now.

48

INTERIOR. CORRIDOR. DAY. TRACKING SHOT.

Two guards move up the corridor. One carries a shoe box full of heroin decks, the other a cigar box for money. Junkie faces at cell doors. Money and heroin pass back and forth. The guards arrive at Dutch's cell. Two junkies buy junk. Dutch watches as the guards pass through a door at the end of the corridor.

Dutch:
There go the smart guys.

49

INTERIOR. CELL. DAY. MEDIUM SHOT.

Squatting on floor of cell, the two junkies cook up together in a tin can. Old junkie looks up at Dutch.

Old Junkie:
Shoot your way to freedom, kid.

ACTION | SOUND

Dutch:
It's pointing the wrong way.

Dutch watches with disgust as they fill eye droppers and roll up their sleeves. The old junkie watches with disapproval as the young junkie ties up for a vein shot.

Old Junkie:
You'll kill yourself that way, kid.

50
INTERIOR. CELLS. DAY. CLOSE-UPS.

Series of shots showing junkies in other cells cooking up, shooting, on the nod, sick and waiting.

51
INTERIOR. HOSPITAL ROOM. DAY. MEDIUM SHOT.

Dutch's voice off-screen:
Sir, please stop it . . . Say, listen, last night . . .

Nurse enters with syringe on a tray. As she bends over the bed to give Dutch a shot of morphine, her face turns into the face of Frances Schultz. Dutch's face is seen. As the shot hits, his face clears.

2nd Detective:
Don't holler.

Voice of Frances Schultz off-screen:
All right dear, you have to get it now.

1st Detective:
Who shot you?

A ventriloquist dummy with monocle, on screen yacking.

Dutch (he speaks quietly at first):
I don't know who can have done it . . . Anybody . . . (*His voice rises.*) They dyed my shoes . . . The Baron says these things . . .

52
INTERIOR. JAIL CORRIDOR. DAY. TRACKING SHOT.

Guards move down corridor with drag queens dressed as famous actresses of the period, their shoes dyed pink, green, blue. Faces at the cell door, teeth bared.

YACKING FALSETTO VOICE OF THE BARON CARRIES OVER AND MIXES WITH TALK OF DRAG QUEENS

Prisoner:
I want Lillian Gish.

Prisoner:
I want Gertrude Lawrence.

Drag queens include Vincent Coll and Albert Stern. Guards open cell doors to let the drag queens in and collect money. The Swede points to a long-haired Filipino boy carrying a red handbag.

Swede:
I want that one.

Nobody wants Albert Stern as Sarah Bernhardt. Just before he goes out with the guards he turns and looks at Dutch, who is standing at cell door.

53
INTERIOR. HOSPITAL ROOM. DAY. MEDIUM SHOT.

Dutch is seen looking at ceiling.

Dutch:
Why can't he just pull out and give me control?

1st Detective:
Do you know who this big fellow was?

54
INTERIOR. CELLS. DAY. CLOSE-UPS.

Dresses, thighs, buttocks.

CHORUS OF ANIMAL NOISES

ACTION | SOUND

55
INTERIOR. CELL. NIGHT. CLOSE-UPS.

Dutch lies on top bunk, looking at
the ceiling. The junk loop and the
sex loop repeat over and over. He
puts a hand to his head.

56
INTERIOR. HOSPITAL ROOM. NIGHT. MEDIUM SHOT.

Voice of Dutch:
My fortunes have changed and come
back and went back since then.
(*His voice rises to a scream.*) It was
desperate. I am wobbly.

1st Detective:
Control yourself.

57
INTERIOR. CELL. DAY. MEDIUM SHOT.

Dutch stands with his back to the cell door. The two junkies are cooking up in a tin can. The Swede has his arm around a drag queen.

Dutch:
Got everything you want in here, don't you? Why don't you settle down and spend the rest of your lives in this creep joint?

Old Junkie:
Take it easy, kid.

Dutch kicks the tin can of heroin solution across the cell. The outraged junkies throw themselves on him. He kicks the young junkie in the shins and knocks the old junkie into the Sicilian's lap. The Sicilian dumps the old junkie to the floor, stands up and hooks Dutch with a left to the stomach, doubling him over. Dutch butts the Sicilian in the face. The Swede knocks him into the arms of guards, who rush in and drag Dutch out.

58
INTERIOR. SOLITARY CELL. DAY. CLOSE-UPS.

Dutch pounds on door and walls. Finally he sits down on bunk, face blank and enigmatic.

59
INTERIOR. CELL. DAY. MEDIUM SHOT.

Guard opens cell door.

Guard:
Here comes a tough one.

Dutch looks around at the hard young faces. Boy on bottom bunk looks at him without moving.

Boy:
Yours is top side.

Dutch:
Who sez?

Boy slides off bunk, a sharpened spring in his hand.

Boy:
I say.

Dutch looks around, calm and confident. These faces will later appear as anonymous gunmen in Dutch Schultz's mob. Dutch smiles. He throws his gear onto the top bunk.

Dutch:
Sure.

60
EXTERIOR. BLACKWELL ISLAND. FERRY DOCK. FALL DAY. MEDIUM SHOT.

Released cons approach the ferry dock with guard. They separate into three categories: addicts, queens, hoodlums. Dutch is with the hoodlum contingent, very reserved and cynical. They board the boat. Old deck hand hoists the gangplank.

Con marginal to Hoodlum group:
Keeps it in a wall safe.

Young Addict:
I'm sick as a dog.

Deck Hand:
I got twelve.

Guard:
Twelve it is. See you sooner, boys.

Con who is trying to make it with Hoodlum group:
This boat take me to the Follies, Pop?

Deck Hand:
It goes to where it came from, kid. Just like you.

61

EXTERIOR. FERRY BOAT. DAY. LONG SHOT.

Clear fall day: late afternoon post-
card shot of New York, a flight of
ducks in the sky. The young addict
is looking at the ducks in the sky.
His face is young looking, owing to
withdrawal, lips parted.

62

EXTERIOR. MISSOURI COUNTRYSIDE. FALL DAY. LONG SHOT.

Leaves changing, a flight of ducks in
the sky.

63

EXTERIOR. SAND BANK BY A STREAM. AFTERNOON. MEDIUM SHOT.

The young addict, transformed into
a healthy college boy is sitting on a
blanket. Beside him is a sophisti-
cated flapper a bit older than he is.
They both follow the ducks across
the sky with their eyes. She raises
a martini glass. "Good luck to them"
in silent movie titles on screen.

Dissolve to evening shadows on
naked bodies. Sex scene.   FROGS CROAKING

64

EXTERIOR. 1920 STREET. DAY. TRACKING SHOT.

Camera follows the paper boy on his
bicycle as he rides up street throw-
ing *The Evening News* on both sides.
We see lawn sprinklers, gardens,
lemonade, boys in white flannels and
blue coats, girls in white dresses, a
woman in a deck chair is reading
If Winter Comes.

ACTION	SOUND

65

EXTERIOR. PICNIC BLANKET BY STREAM. EVENING. MEDIUM SHOT.

Sex scene repeats.

66

EXTERIOR. VIEW OF A DISTANT COUNTRY CLUB. NIGHT. LONG SHOT.

The country club is seen across
water.   DISTANT MUSIC, SAXOPHONES

67

EXTERIOR. PICNIC. EVENING. MEDIUM SHOT.

Sex scene repeats.

68

EXTERIOR. TRAIN THROUGH WINTER LANDSCAPE. EVENING. LONG SHOT.

Steam train.   TRAIN WHISTLE

69

INTERIOR. TRAIN STATION. EVENING. MEDIUM SHOT.

Boy gets off train with suitcase. Thin
boy in prep school clothes. He looks
about expectantly. Porter turns.
Badge No. 23.

70

EXTERIOR. PICNIC. SUNSET. MEDIUM SHOT.

Sex scene is cut-in with shots of
Pikes Peak, Grand Canyon, Niagara
Falls, rainbow.

71

INTERIOR. HOSPITAL ROOM. EVENING. MEDIUM SHOT.

Post card shot of the Old Harmony
Hotel.

Voice of Dutch:
I don't want harmony. I want harmony . . . John, please . . . oh, did
you buy the hotel?

72

INTERIOR. CORRIDOR. DAY. MEDIUM SHOT.

Ghostly scene shows phantom porter
walking away from the camera down
a long hall.

PORTER WHISTLES "HOME SWEET
HOME"

73

INTERIOR. OFFICE. DAY. MEDIUM SHOT.

Hard-faced, middle-aged Irish man
with cigar. Two young hoodlums
stand in front of the desk. This is
silent film with written titles. "The
pay is fifty clams a week. You want
the job?" The hoodlums nod. The
man slides two guns across the desk.
"You'll be needing these."

74

INTERIOR. GARAGE. NIGHT. MEDIUM SHOT.

The two hoodlums stand by a beer
truck.
1st hoodlum: "Oh, boy! Fifty bucks
a week!"
2nd hoodlum: "I wonder what he
makes?"

75
EXTERIOR. ROAD. NIGHT. MEDIUM SHOTS.

Hijacking shots, windshields shot
out, trucks overturning, spilling beer
kegs.

76
INTERIOR. OFFICE. NIGHT. MEDIUM SHOT.

The hard-faced man is on the phone.
"I got a smart punk here."
He looks up to see shadow of young
hoodlums with machine gun.

77
EXTERIOR. FRONT OF CHURCH. DAY. MEDIUM SHOT.

Gangster wedding, bride and groom
flanked by bodyguards, black Cadil-

lac waiting. A manhole cover pops up in a cloud of steam and the two young hoodlums mow down the wedding guests.

78
EXTERIOR. CEMETERY. DAY. MEDIUM SHOT.

Gangster funeral: mourners and bodyguards. The coffin flies open and the two guns drop the mourners among the tombstones.

79
EXTERIOR. STREET. DAY. MEDIUM SHOT.

Disguised as old ladies in an electric the two guns mow down mobsters.

80
INTERIOR. BEER DROP. DAY. TRACKING SHOT.

The successful mobster walks through a vast beer drop giving orders and checking accounts. These scenes are stock, and stock footage can be used—would in fact be preferable. This must look like a 1920 film.

81
EXTERIOR. FERRY BOAT. EVENING. MEDIUM SHOT.

The boat is about to dock. The released cons stream to the prow of the boat. A dog is barking intermittently on the landing pier. The old deck hand appears.

Old Deck Hand:
You fellows can't stay in the bow when we dock.

A DOG BARKS CALMLY. IT IS NOT HOS-
TILE OR ASSERTIVE; IT JUST SAYS, THIS
IS ME THIS IS ME.

Hoodlums:
Who sez?

ASSERTIVE HOSTILE BARK BASICALLY
UNSURE OF POSITION

*Old Deck Hand (very cool and re-
mote):*
It's the rules.

DISTANT DOG BARKS FROM A 1920
GARDEN

*The officious con (who does most
of the talking on occasions like this.
It's an old Army type, too):*
Wait a minute, Pop. I remember last
time I rode this tub. Anybody got
a coupla quarters?

AN OBSEQUIOUS, BLACKMAILING BARK
YOU DON'T GET RID OF ME THAT EASY,
SNARLS THE CHAUFFEUR, EYES SUD-
DENLY VICIOUS IN HIS THIN, RED, ACNE-
SCARRED FACE. IT'S A FRONT-OFFICE
BROWN-NOSE BARK, FAWNING AND
SNARLING, IT'S AN INFORMER'S BARK
(If this seems to demand too much
of our canine actors, they know their
parts since dogs left their wild in-
nocence to mooch on mankind they
hoped and can readily be recorded
in any area where the species
abounds. All the archetypical canine
artists can be recorded in Tangiers.)

One of the drag queens, very wan
and young looking in a suit too big
for him, hands the con two quarters.

PLAINTIVE BARK FROM A DESERTED
VILLA

Officious Con:
Here, do that trick you did before,
Pop.

The old deck hand takes the coins and puts them in his eyes. Fear flickers for a split second in every face except the officious con. This is his moment. Most of the cons laugh self-consciously. Dutch's face is ugly.

Old Deck Hand:
I don't see nothing.

He pockets the coins and ambles away.

82
INTERIOR. HOSPITAL ROOM. DAY. MEDIUM SHOT.

Detective starts at the sudden shrill warning.

Voice of Dutch:
Look out. Look out for him. He changed for the worse.
STEADY BARK SHOWS QUARRY HAS BEEN LOCATED

The detective recovers his composure. His face is ugly.

Detective:
What did they shoot you for?

Voice of Dutch (his voice is distant):
Fire . . . factory he was nowhere near it smoldered . . .

On screen, factory fire and smoldering ruins, gutted rooms.

83
EXTERIOR. FAÇADE OF OTTO GRASS REMOVALS AND STORAGE. DAY. MEDIUM SHOT.

Dutch and Joe Noe look at the name and address. This is silent film with printed leads.

Dutch: "This must be it."

30

84
INTERIOR. OTTO GRASS'S OFFICE. DAY. MEDIUM SHOT.

Joe and Dutch stand in front of the desk.

Otto: "We're not moving furniture now. We're moving something else."

Dutch: "Like what?"

Otto: "Like beer. The pay is fifty clams a week. You want the job?"

Dutch and Joe: "Sure."

Otto: "You'll be needing these."

He slides the guns across the desk. This identical scene is played by different actors.

THE SOUND TRACK IS SHUT OFF IN THIS SCENE. (That is, it is not just an absence of sound *on* the track but the track itself which is off.)

85
ON SCREEN IN GOLDEN LETTERS:

"It is more profitable to give wages than to receive them."

SOUND TRACK BACK ON

Voice of Dutch off-screen:
My gilt-edge stuff and those dirty rats have tuned in . . .

HOSPITAL SOUND EFFECTS

86
INTERIOR. GARAGE BEHIND SPEAKEASY. DAY. MEDIUM SHOT.

Dutch, Joe Noe, Bo Weinberg watch as Vincent and Peter Coll and Fats Columbo get in rickety beer truck. Vincent and Peter Coll are country Irish, surly and vicious. Vincent is the more volatile of the two. Fats Columbo is soft and degenerate look-

---

ing, with pale, dead eyes. A horrible trio.

Fats is at the wheel. The two Coll brothers riding shotgun. A middle-aged Negro opens the door. The truck rattles out.

87

INTERIOR. BEER DROP. NIGHT. MEDIUM SHOT.

Beer truck is being loaded. We see the interior of the beer drop, the guards, the office. The door opens and the truck rattles out.

88

EXTERIOR. ROAD. NIGHT. MEDIUM SHOT.

Truck across the road in headlights. As the truck slows down the Coll brothers throw up a trap door in the roof of the cab and stand up, pump shotguns blazing. Three hijackers crumple. Expressionless Fats rams the cab of the truck, spinning it aside, and drives through.

SHOTS, SHOUTS, MOTOR SOUNDS

89
INTERIOR. BEER DROP. NIGHT. MEDIUM SHOT.

Dutch, Bo Weinberg, Joe Noe and a number of new guns. A line of trucks and an escort truck with benches and twelve guns, among them the Colls. The trucks move out. Dutch is checking accounts.

Dutch:
And don't fall for any cop suits.

90
INTERIOR. NIGHTCLUB. OFFICE. NIGHT. MEDIUM SHOT.

Legs Diamond sits in padded armchair, completely immobile. Backdrop is the archetypical mobster's nightclub office: wall safes, liquor cabinets, submachine guns in the closet, etc. His lips do not move.

Voice of Legs Diamond (a malignant, cold, hissing, snake sound):
Now, about this whatsisname? Flegenheimer Sheenie won't stay uptown . . .

91
INTERIOR. SAME NIGHTCLUB OFFICE. NIGHT. MEDIUM SHOT.

Dutch and Legs Diamond stand facing each other in the middle of the office. Dutch is flanked by Bo Weinberg and Joe Noe. Behind Legs stand two Dominican guns with smooth, tight faces. Legs is very much a Rubirosa type—smooth, cold, reptilian, with a charm irresistible as the fear his presence inspires. Dutch and his entourage look like stolid Dutch bankers in the house of an Italian prince. Bo Weinberg calm, solid, unimpressed. Dutch is a little slow for Diamond, but steadier and solider. Legs has more style, but Dutch has more staying power.

33

ACTION	SOUND

Legs Diamond:
I think we can agree in principle, Mr Flegenheimer. As you pointed out, you have the beer and the drops. Why go to Jersey for our beer? Fine. Thank you. Let's all sit down and drink to that.

Dutch is a bit put out by this disconcerting speech, and not at all sure what he is drinking to. The drinks are served by a middle-aged Negro who will later appear as one of Dutch's guns. Dutch raises his glass. The gun sits with glass in left hand.

Dutch:
I thought you'd see it like that.

Legs Diamond:
I do. There are other people involved. I think that can be arranged, Flegenheimer. Don't you have a moniker? A name people will remember thirty, forty, a hundred years from now?

Joe Noe:
Some people call him Dutch.

Legs Diamond:
How about Dutch Schultz? You remember him, Dutch? Old welterweight did time for a payroll heist.

Dutch:
Dutch Schultz . . . Hmmmm, yes I like that.

Legs Diamond:
It will take me a few days to cool this and wrap it up. Suppose we get together for lunch early next week? Say Tuesday. One o'clock at Ciro's? You know the place?

Dutch:
We were hoping for a definite answer now, Legs.

ACTION	SOUND

Legs Diamond:
It's not possible on such short notice. Bo knows that.

Bo Weinberg:
He's right about that, Dutch.

92
EXTERIOR. PARKING LOT. MILD, FOGGY GREY DAY. MEDIUM SHOT.

Dutch, Bo Weinberg and Joe Noe get out of a car.

AIR HAMMERS, FOG HORNS

Dutch:
He won't try anything in a restaurant . . .

93
EXTERIOR. STREET. DAY. TRACKING SHOT.

Long street—warehouses and machine shops on one side, the other side under demolition: walls sheared off, exposing the rooms with paper on the walls. Halfway down the block a sign: MEN WORKING. An air hammer. As the camera approaches, we see that the worker with the air hammer is one of Legs's Dominican guns. The other gun steps out from behind the compressor˙ and opens up with machine gun. Joe Noe falls. Bo Weinberg sweeps Dutch into a doorway. They draw pistols and fire. The gun collapses over the air hammer, which now vibrates. Blood out of his mouth, his limp face out of focus. A burst pins Dutch and Bo in doorway, and a final burst goes into the body of Joe Noe. The gun fades into the gutted buildings.

SOUND OF AIR HAMMER LOUDER AND LOUDER

THE GUNFIRE CANNOT BE HEARD ABOVE THE AIR HAMMER

94

INTERIOR–EXTERIOR. WALL STREET 1929. DAY. MEDIUM SHOTS.

Stock footage of 1929 crash which are cut-in with the following scenes.

95

EXTERIOR. FRONT OF STOCK EXCHANGE. DAY. MEDIUM SHOT.

An old black Packard stops and the ghostly figure of Hetty Green gets out. No one else sees her as she walks up the steps.

Old Runner:
Hetty Green, the Witch of Wall Street.

96

INTERIOR. STOCK EXCHANGE. DAY. MEDIUM SHOT.

Hetty Green stands at the center of the Stock Exchange. She turns in a little jig. Her lips do not move.

She twists faster and faster.

Voice of Hetty Green:
Ding dong bell. Sell. Sell. Sell. Sell.
Sig Boom fell. Old Tower fell. Tele Con Polaroid Mutter spell fell. Vornado pell mell. SELL SELL SELL.

She disappears in a black funnel, her voice the scream of wind across the dust bowl, skeletons of cattle and empty farms.

97
EXTERIOR. WALL STREET. DAY. MEDIUM SHOT.

Brokers and ruined investors hurtle
toward the sidewalk. Explosion of
blood and guts in color.

98
INTERIOR. ROOM. NIGHT. MEDIUM SHOT.

Sex scene between red-haired boy
and Bennington girl. A typical
Greenwhich Village set of the
period. Communist posters on the
wall. The sex scene is cut-in with
book burnings, the Red flag, apples
in a basket, a window display for
lipstick with a bust of Egyptian
princess.

99

EXTERIOR. FRONT OF THE LIPSTICK WINDOW DISPLAY. DAY.
MEDIUM SHOT.

Dutch turns aside the apple peddler.
Picture returns to black and white.
He is standing with Bo Weinberg
and George Weinberg.

Paper Boy:
Read all about it! . . . Legs Diamond aquitted! . . . Paper, mister?

STOCKS COLLAPSE IN 16,410,030-SHARE DAY, BUT RALLY AT CLOSE CHEERS BROKERS; BANKERS OPTIMISTIC, TO CONTINUE AID

Dutch takes a paper and hands the
boy a dollar.

Paper Boy:
I don't have change, mister.

Dutch:
Did I ask you for any change?

Boy walks away.

Paper Boy:
Gee, thanks, mister. . . . Read all
about it. . . . Legs Diamond acquitted! . . .

100

INTERIOR. PHONE BOOTH. NIGHT. CLOSE-UP.

Legs Diamond in phone booth.
Legs is older, shabbier and his
smooth confidence is gone. He is
quite drunk. There is a raw urgency
in his face and voice.

SOUND EFFECTS OF NOISY PARTY

Legs Diamond:
Kiki? This is Legs. I wanta see you.

Kiki (with a cool, creamy laugh):
All right, Jack . . . in twenty min-
utes.

101
INTERIOR. HOTEL ROOM. NIGHT. MEDIUM SHOT.

Three guns playing rummy . . . The
middle-aged Negro who served the
drinks in Legs's office; the red-haired
boy who plays in sex scenes—older
cool and alert; a pock-marked shrew-
faced Latin. The phone cradled, he
continues the rummy game.

Red-Haired Gun:
Yeah?

KIKI'S VOICE

An hour be time enough?

KIKI'S VOICE

Keys? No, that won't be necessary.

KIKI'S VOICE

O.K. O.K.

ACTION	SOUND

102
EXTERIOR. STREET CORNER. NIGHT. LONG SHOT.

Dove Street . . . bleak shot of shabby rooming houses.

103
INTERIOR. ROOMING HOUSE. STAIRS. NIGHT. TRACKING SHOT.

Legs is stumbling up the stairs, pulling himself along the banister. His overcoat is open and his face wears an expression of bestial urgency.

104
INTERIOR. ROOM. NIGHT. MEDIUM SHOT.

Kiki stands in the shabby front room. Legs drops his overcoat on a chair. They go into a passionate embrace.

Kiki:
You *are* in a hurry.

105
INTERIOR. NIGHT. BEDROOM. CLOSE-UP.

Sex scene between Kiki and Legs. Her face is a mask of evil ecstasy. As sex scene reaches a climax, the screen goes dark.

SOUND OF DRUNKEN SLEEP

106
EXTERIOR. DOVE STREET. NIGHT. LONG SHOT.

Kiki comes out a door and walks down Dove Street.

107
INTERIOR. BEDROOM. NIGHT. CLOSE-UP.

Legs asleep on the crumpled bed, his face smeared with lipstick. He sits up groggily and looks around. Bullets hit his chest and face.

KEY IN LOCK

Legs Diamond:
Kiki? Huh? Who is it?

108
INTERIOR. OFFICE OF BEER DROP. DAY. MEDIUM SHOT.

Dutch, Bo Weinberg, and George Weinberg in office. Dutch reaches for his lumpy overcoat.

Dutch:
We still have slot machines . . .

109
INTERIOR. SLOT MACHINE. DAY. CLOSE-UP.

Slot machine jumps off jackpot.

110
INTERIOR. OFFICE. DAY. MEDIUM SHOT.

Dutch has one arm through the
overcoat.

Dutch:
And small loans.

111
EXTERIOR. STREET. NIGHT. MEDIUM SHOT.

Man walking down street. Two
figures step from the doorway. A
thin, rat-faced man and a hulking
giant.

Thin Man:
Haven't you forgotten something
you should remember?

Man:
Brutal beating follows.

I tell you I can't pay.

112
INTERIOR. OFFICE. DAY. MEDIUM SHOT.

Dutch is buttoning his overcoat.

Dutch:
And protection . . .

113
INTERIOR. BAR. NIGHT. MEDIUM SHOT.

Well-dressed patrons exude wealth
and self-possession. Two men sta-
tioned at the middle of the bar seem
somewhat out of place. One has long
powerful arms and prominent cheek
bones. He looks like Mr Hyde. The
other wears a frozen, blank expression. A patron at the end of the bar
turns to his companion.

Patron:
Embassy people, I think.

Standing by this pair, a millionaire,
warmed by three martinis, looks at

them as if trying to focus, to remember at what house party or reception . . . The patrons start back. Mr Hyde sweeps a row of glasses to the floor. The frozen-faced hoodlum, without changing his expression, grabs an elegant young man by the lapels and shoves him across the room, where he overturns a table and lands in the lap of an aristocratic, bejeweled woman.

Mr Hyde:
What are you looking at?

114
INTERIOR. DINING ROOM. NIGHT. MEDIUM SHOT.

Slowly, conversation dies and the guests stop eating. A pink-faced, middle-aged guest sitting with his wife and daughter puts down his knife and fork.

Pink-Faced Guest:
Mother, this place stinks.

115
INTERIOR. CLOAKROOM. NIGHT. CLOSE-UP.

Woman is helped into her mink coat by the hat check girl. The woman preens herself, then sniffs and stiffens and looks down. The bottom of her coat is in rags, steaming red and orange fumes. A blob of smoking fur falls to the floor.

SHE SCREAMS LIKE A STRICKEN BABY

116
EXTERIOR. FRONT OF WOOLWORTH'S. DAY. MEDIUM SHOT.

Dutch, Bo Weinberg, and George Weinberg. This is uptown Woolworth's, Negro and Puerto Rican patrons in and out.

Dutch:
And numbers . . .

Bo Weinberg:
That's nickels and dimes.

Dutch:
Nickels and dimes add up.

117
EXTERIOR. FRONT OF WOOLWORTH'S. DAY. LONG SHOT.

Same scene seen from a distance, progressively underexposed, darkness seeping in.

HOSPITAL SOUND EFFECTS

118
STILL PHOTO ON BACK PLATFORM OF ROYAL PALM SPECIAL. LEFT TO RIGHT: PETER COLL, VINCENT COLL, FATS COLUMBO.

119
INTERIOR. TRAIN DRAWING ROOM. EVENING. MEDIUM SHOT.

Vincent and Peter Coll and Fats Columbo seated at table with bottle of whiskey. The train is traveling at high speed, lurching, the windows rattling. Soot drifts across the table. Through the window we see a summer landscape flash by.

DURING THIS SCENE THE CLICKING OF TRAIN WHEELS (CLICKETY-CLACK), THE TRAIN WHISTLE (WHOO WHOO), THE WHOOSH OF A TRAIN IN THE OPPOSITE DIRECTION, OR A TRAIN ENTERING A TUNNEL, CUTS THE VOICES OF THE ACTORS

Vincent Coll:
I mean, how did the Dutchman (WHOO WHOO) where he is? By carrying (CLICKETY-CLACK) for some one else? (WHOO WHOO)

Fats Columbo:
That's right. We take the risks in the (CLICKETY-CLACK)

The train sways, and Fats grabs for his whiskey glass.

The Dutchman grabs the (WHOO WHOO)

ACTION	SOUND

Peter Coll:
If we start (CLICKETY-CLACK) on our own we'll have the Dutchman's (CLICKETY-CLACK) all over us.

Vincent Coll:
Why wait for (CLICKETY-CLACK) Why not (CLICKETY-CLACK) first?

Fats Columbo:
The Dutchman underpays his (CLICKETY-CLACK) and chisels his (WHOOSH OF TRAIN ENTERING TUNNEL) If we could offer a better (CLICKETY-CLACK)

Vincent Coll:
We gotta hit his key (WHOO WHOO) Show what we can do and his (CLICKETY-CLACK, WHOOSH OF TRAIN IN OPPOSITE DIRECTION) will come over

Coll clutches his chest. A sudden lurch of the train throws him back in his seat. A glass crashes to the floor.

(Complete sentences are as follows:)

Vincent Coll:
I mean, how did the Dutchman get where he is? By carrying gun for someone else?

Fats Columbo:
That's right. We take the risks in the street and the Dutchman grabs the lard.

Peter Coll:
If we start business on our own we'll have the Dutchman's guns all over us.

Vincent Coll:
Why wait for his hit? Why not hit him first?

Fats Columbo:
The Dutchman underpays his guns and chisels his runners. If we could offer a better deal . . .

47

ACTION	SOUND

Vincent Coll:
We gotta hit his key men. Show what we can do and his key men will come over . . .

Through the train window, camera picks out boy with a dog, waving to the train. Camera zooms in on the boy, lifts audience out of train to . . .

120
EXTERIOR. HILLSIDE. EVENING. MEDIUM SHOT.

Boy with his dog waves to the train.   TRAIN WHISTLE, FROGS CROAKING

121
SAME BOY WITH DOG WAVING TO TRAIN ON "SATURDAY EVENING POST" COVER.

122
BOYS FISHING, SWIMMING, CLIMBING TREES, EVENING SHADOWS ON THE OLD SWIMMING HOLE.

HOSPITAL SOUND EFFECTS

123
EXTERIOR. STREET. EVENING. MEDIUM SHOT.

Children playing in the street. The girls are in pink and light blue dresses, the boys in shorts and colored shirts. A middle-class street. Apartment door. Doorman is one of the guards from the prison scenes. Joey Rao emerges with two bodyguards. He nods to the doorman, who touches his cap. Rao is a smooth, plump Latin who walks with a slow, stately gait, threading

his way through children and baby
carriages. He nods to acquaintances,
stops by a baby carriage, and looks
down. The bodyguards fall behind,
yawning. Boy who waved to train
releases a red balloon. Shading his
eyes he watches as the balloon sails
up past apartment windows.

Rao:
Buenas tardes, jovencita.

124
INTERIOR. CAR. EVENING. MEDIUM SHOT.

A battered black Packard halfway
down the block. The radiator steams.
Fats Columbo is at the wheel.
Vincent and Peter Coll are in the
back seat. Vincent Coll has a machine gun in his lap.
The car draws abreast of Rao. Suddenly a pillar of steam from the
overheated radiator blows back
across the windshield, cutting Columbo's view. The car swerves
wildly.

Vincent Coll:
That's Rao. Let's go.

125
EXTERIOR. STREET. EVENING. LONG SHOT.

Boy watches as balloon clears the
roof tops.

126
INTERIOR–EXTERIOR. CAR. EVENING. MEDIUM SHOT.

Speeding, swerving car. Coll leans
out the back window and sprays the
block with machine-gun bullets.
Peter Coll leans over beside him and
empties a revolver.

SHOTS

49

127
EXTERIOR. STREET. EVENING. MEDIUM SHOT.

Boy's white shirt splashed with red. He brings down hand that shaded his eyes, clutches stomach, and crumples forward. Four other children falling. Blood, pink dresses, splintered peppermint candy, crushed ice-cream cones.

SHOTS, SCREAMS

128
EXTERIOR. DOORWAY. EVENING. MEDIUM SHOT.

Rao and his bodyguards, standing in a doorway, survey the scene with shocked incredulity and disapproval as if someone had exposed himself in public.

ACTION | SOUND

129
EXTERIOR. STREET. EVENING. LONG SHOT.

Car swerves around corner and disappears with a last glimpse of the
snarling Coll brothers.

130
EXTERIOR. SKY. EVENING. LONG SHOT.

Red balloon, blue sky streamers of
pink cloud.

131
INTERIOR. HOTEL ROOM. NIGHT. MEDIUM SHOT.

Four mobsters smoking opium in a
dimly-lit room. The pipe is a bottle
with pinhole and a rubber tube.
Scene is hermetic, reptilian.

Voices of the Colls off-screen:
This is a dope raid.

The door crashes open. Vincent
sprays the recumbent mobsters with
machine-gun bullets.

132
INTERIOR. OFFICE. DAY. MEDIUM SHOT.

Desk phone, filing cabinets. Office
looks like moderately successful
businessman's. Dutch, Bo Weinberg,
Lulu Rosencrantz, Abe Landau. A
seedy little man stands in front of
the desk, with his hat in his hands.
This is the same actor who played
the officious con in the ferry boat
scene.

Bo Weinberg:
Tell him what you told me.

Messenger:
Now look, Mr Flegenheimer, this is
just what I *hear* . . . I mean, what
Vincent Coll is saying all over
town . . .

ACTION	SOUND

Dutch:
All right what's he saying?

Messenger:
He's, uh, well, he's calling you a yellow rat, Mr Flegenheimer. He's saying if you aren't yellow, why don't you come out in the open and fight?

Dutch (smiling):
Now who does he think he is? Wyatt Earp or somebody?

Messenger:
It's just what I hear, Mr Flegenheimer.

Dutch walks over and puts a hand on the messenger's shoulder.

Dutch (genially):
That's all right. Now listen. I want you to put it out on the grapevine that I'm willing to sit down with Coll and his boys and talk things over and see if we can't come to a fair agreement. You understand?

Messenger:
Yes, Mr Flegenheimer. I got it. I'll put the word out. You can depend on me.

Dutch:
Good. Show him out the back way, Lulu.

Exit Lulu with messenger.

Bo Weinberg:
He's not that dumb, Dutch.

Dutch:
Of course not. But it puts me in the right. I offered to sit down with him like a gentleman and talk things over, and he didn't want to listen . . . Meanwhile we'll stay under-cover until this situation is handled.

133
INTERIOR. APARTMENT ROOM. NIGHT. MEDIUM SHOT.

Five Schultz mobsters are playing Monopoly on a specially constructed enlarged board with model hotels, garages, jails, banks.

134
INTERIOR. CORRIDOR. NIGHT. MEDIUM SHOT.

Smoke bomb explodes in corridor.

135
INTERIOR. ROOM. NIGHT. MEDIUM SHOT.

Monopoly game still going on.

Mobster:
I smell smoke.

A fire ax through the door. The door buckles and flies open. In the space vacated by the shattered door stand Vincent Coll and Fats Columbo in fireman uniforms. They open up with machine guns. The mobsters fall across the Monopoly board, model properties clutched in dying fingers.

Voice of Coll off-screen:
Fire department . . .

SHOTS

136
INTERIOR. BEER DROP. NIGHT. MEDIUM SHOT.

Vincent and Peter Coll, and Fats Columbo are wrecking the premises in a frenzy of vandalism. With sledge hammers and iron bars they smash slot machines and beer trucks. They slosh gasoline on the floor and leave in a whoosh of flame.

BANGING
FIRE ENGINES

137
INTERIOR. APARTMENT ROOM. NIGHT. MEDIUM SHOT.

This is the same apartment hide-out Dutch will later use when dodging arrest for income-tax evasion. Dutch, Lulu Rosencrantz, Abe Landau, Bo and George Weinberg, the Negro gun, the red-haired gun, the shrew-faced gun. Dutch stands with the phone in his hands. He cuts connection and calls another number.

Dutch:
They just wrecked the College Avenue drop. I was wondering if you could lend me some talent. I'm a bit shorthanded on this show.

138
INTERIOR. NIGHTCLUB OFFICE. NIGHT. CLOSE-UP.

FAINT MUSIC OFF-SCREEN

Mobster picks up phone.

Mobster:
Sorry Dutch. He's your boy.

139
INTERIOR. APARTMENT. NIGHT. MEDIUM SHOT.

Dutch turns from the phone to his loyal guns.

Dutch:
Get Coll off my back! Get the Mick off my back!

Bo Weinberg:
He's hard to find, Dutch.

Dutch sits down and pours a drink.

Dutch:
He's hard to find, but he finds others . . . (*His face lights up.*) Owney Maddon is a queer . . . used to be sweet on Coll. (*He takes a long swallow and continues philosophically.*) When a queer gets the hots he don't think what he's getting into. Coll will bleed Owney for the last

54

ACTION	SOUND

He points to the red-haired gun and the shrew-faced gun.

nickel . . . (*He puts down empty glass.*) You and you follow Owney. Don't let him out of your sight. Stick with Owney till you find that creep . . . Can you lay ona wire-tap, George?

George Weinberg:
Can do, Dutch . . . garage right down the street from Owney's . . . We got a girl in the exchange to trace calls . . .

Dutch:
Good. And you (*he points to the Negro gun*) find his potato-eating brother.

Negro Gun:
I'll find him, Mr Flegenheimer.

140
EXTERIOR. STREET. EARLY MORNING. MEDIUM SHOT.

Peter Coll stands in the doorway of a speakeasy, a stubble of beard on his slow-witted surly face.
He looks up the street to his right. The street is empty. He looks to his left. Street is empty except for an old Negro trash collector with a wagon. He is emptying trash receptacles from lampposts into his cart. He moves very slowly as if crippled. Coll looks at him, looks away to the right and steps from the doorway. As he faces to the right and is about to walk in that direction an expression of bestial suspicion clouds his face. He pivots to the left and walks over to Negro trash collector.

He pokes around in the cart.

Peter Coll:
What you got in those cans, George?

	ACTION	SOUND

SOUND

Negro Gun:
Just trash is all, boss.

Peter Coll:
Thought it might be something else . . .

Negro Gun:
You a copper, mister?

Peter Coll (*he thinks this over for a second and decides it is a good idea*): Yeah. Looking for dope. Watch your step.

ACTION

Peter Coll turns away and walks to the right. The Negro gun, now lithe and quick, steps forward and slips a sawed-off shotgun from a trash container.

Negro Gun:
Yes sir, I certainly will do that. Yes sir, Mister Coll . . .

141
EXTERIOR. STREET. MORNING. CLOSE-UP.

Shot of Coll's face as this sinks in. It is already the face of a corpse.

142
EXTERIOR. STREET. MORNING. MEDIUM SHOT.

Negro gun fires both barrels. Double load of buckshot pitches Coll forward.

143
INTERIOR. GARAGE. DAY. MEDIUM SHOT.

Bo Weinberg, Jimmy the Shrew, the red-haired gun, an anonymous grey gun who looks like an FBI man, a technician. The technician wearing steel-rimmed glasses and head-phones is making adjustments at a switchboard. This is the same actor who plays the police stenographer. He takes off headphones. He removes plugs, filing off the insulation with a knife. The red-haired gun is reading *Weird Tales*. On the cover is a tentacled monster with a human face. *Abooth the Unclean*. Bo Weinberg is studying a racing form. The grey gun and Jimmy the Shrew are junkies, and sit there doing absolutely nothing.

Red-haired gun, magazine folded over finger, picks up the phone.

Technician:
I'm getting every fart on the block.

PHONE RINGS

Red-Haired Gun:
Yeah, he called twice, but he rings off before we can trace it . . .

DUTCH'S VOICE
O.K. Dutch. Will do.

A light flashes on the switchboard.

144
INTERIOR. NIGHTCLUB OFFICE. DAY. MEDIUM SHOT.

Owney Maddon picks up phone.

Owney:
Oh hello, Vincent.

145
INTERIOR. GARAGE. DAY. MEDIUM SHOT.

Technician puts on headphones. He raises a finger. The guns stand up. Bo and the grey gun pick up submachine guns. The red-haired gun picks up a bunch of skeleton keys.

146
INTERIOR. OFFICE. DAY. MEDIUM SHOT.

Red-haired gun stands behind Maddon, his gun drawn.

Red-Haired Gun:
Keep talking, Owney. Stall him.

Owney Maddon glances up without
surprise, and nods. Perhaps he has
known about the wiretap. He wants
the Mick off his back, too.

Owney:
Be reasonable, Vincent . . .

COLL'S VOICE
I tell you, I just don't have that kind
of money.

147
INTERIOR. GARAGE. DAY. MEDIUM SHOT.

Technician is busy at the switchboard. Jimmy the Shrew is at the
wheel of car, motor running. Bo
Weinberg and the grey gun in back
seat.

148
INTERIOR. TELEPHONE EXCHANGE. DAY. MEDIUM SHOT.

Kiki Robberts in front of switchboard, chewing gum. She is plugging
in switches.

CLICKS, BUZZES, BITS OF CONVERSATION
ACTUAL RECORDINGS OF TELEPHONE
SOUND

149
INTERIOR. GARAGE. DAY. MEDIUM SHOT.

The technician takes off headphones.
The Shrew leans a jug ear out of the
car.

ACTION	SOUND

Technician:
Drugstore phone booth. Corner 23rd
Street and 10th Avenue.

150
INTERIOR. OFFICE. DAY. MEDIUM SHOT.

Owney:
Business is falling off, and I took a
beating on my income tax.

151
EXTERIOR. STREET. DAY. MEDIUM SHOT.

Car with guns weaving through
traffic.

152
INTERIOR. OFFICE. DAY. MEDIUM SHOT.

As Owney talks, he glances up from
time to time coquettishly at the red-
haired gun.

Owney:
Well, I might be able to raise ten
thousand, Vincent . . . It would
mean selling shares at a loss . . .

COLL'S VOICE

153
EXTERIOR. FRONT OF DRUGSTORE. DAY. MEDIUM SHOT.

Car stops in front of the drugstore.
The Shrew stays at the wheel. Bo
Weinberg and grey gun get out and
go in store.

154
INTERIOR. DRUGSTORE. DAY. MEDIUM SHOT.

Grey gun takes station at door, gun held six inches below level position. He raises the gun an inch. Druggist ducks behind counter. Bo Weinberg walks over to phone booth and opens up at six feet.

Gun:
On the floor, Pop.

MACHINE-GUN SHOTS

155
INTERIOR. OFFICE. DAY. MEDIUM SHOT.

Owney Maddon holds the phone away from his ear for the red-haired gun to hear. He puts the phone down.

MACHINE-GUN SHOTS ON PHONE

Owney:
Ever think about getting out of it, kid?

(The following shots of Harlem in the 1930s can use any available documentary material of the period and place. This not only saves expensive reconstruction but gives the background shots more authenticity.)

156
EXTERIOR. TWILIGHT. HARLEM STREET CORNER. MEDIUM SHOT.

This scene is dark and underexposed. The Harlem shots convey an impression of twilight world of phantoms. Newspaper stand on corner. A few pedestrians walk by and drop two cents for a paper. One stops and opens paper.

157
CLOSE-UP OF FRONT PAGE SHOWS THE SIGN AT 23rd AND 10th . . .
"VINCENT COLL, AGE 23, OF 228 WEST 23rd STREET"

Flashback of the car stopping, Coll sprawling out of the telephone booth as a black hand writes 23223 down on policy slip.

MACHINE-GUN SHOTS

158

CLOSE-UP OF NEWSPAPER. "23 DIE IN APARTMENT HOUSE BLAST."

Flash of fire, people screaming at
windows, as hands—black brown
white—write variations of 23.   SCREAMS, FIRE ENGINES

159

CLOSE-UP OF NEWSPAPER. "COMMON-LAW WIFE HE SLEW
STABBING HER 23 TIMES."

Shot of stabbing as hands write variations of 23.   SCREAMS, SPANISH CURSES

160

CAMERA PICKS OUT NUMBERS, STREET SIGNS, AND ADDRESSES,
PRICES IN SHOP WINDOWS, POLICE AND FIREMAN BADGES.
A SKULL-FACED PORTER TURNS AROUND. THE NUMBER ON HIS CAP
IS 23. A SCREEN OF NUMBERS SUPERIMPOSED ON HARLEM SHOTS.

161

EXTERIOR. STREET. TWILIGHT. MEDIUM SHOT.

Runner picking up slips and paying
off the winning numbers. Preferably
an actual runner should be located
for this sequence.

162

EXTERIOR. STREET. TWILIGHT. MEDIUM SHOT.

Runner stopped by the red-haired
gun, the Negro gun, a Puerto Rican
gun.

Negro Gun:
Like to talk to you a minute.

Harlem background shots are cut-
in and blank out guns and runner
so that we hear the words intermittently.

Red-Haired Gun:
33 percent.

Background shots.

Puerto Rican Gun:
Protection.

Background shots.

Negro Gun:
Come in with the Dutchman.

Pictures of Dutch cut-in with Harlem background shots.

163
INTERIOR. HOTEL CORRIDOR. NIGHT. MEDIUM SHOT.

Three guns in front of room 33. Redhaired gun opens door with skeleton keys in left hand. He slips silencered automatic from shoulder holster and goes in.

WHO IS IT? SPUT SPUT SPUT

164
EXTERIOR. STREET. TWILIGHT. MEDIUM SHOT.

Runner stopped by three different guns as Dutch's army of guns grows. Same words and same cut-ins are used in this shot. "33 percent and protection," "Come in with the Dutchman."

165
INTERIOR. OFFICE. DAY. MEDIUM SHOT.

Fat Negro taking down numbers as his runners phone in. Gun is doing crossword puzzle.

166
INTERIOR. LOFT ROOM. DAY. MEDIUM SHOT.

The technician drinks a bicarbonate of soda and belches into his hand. He puts on headphones. A Chinese gun with tinted glasses is reading a girlie magazine with a completely expressionless face. A young black gun is playing with a yo-yo. The technician raises a finger.

167
EXTERIOR. STREET. TWILIGHT. MEDIUM SHOT.

The standout policy boss and two guns. Car pulls up and stops. The Chinese gun takes them one after the other with a silencered rifle.

SPUT SPUT SPUT

168
EXTERIOR. STREETS. TWILIGHT. MEDIUM SHOTS.

Guns stopping runners.

Dutch's picture intercut is larger and larger until it covers the screen. This shot is stylized with a hint of song and dance. In last shot we see the young gun with yo-yo.

AN ARMY OF GUNS ONE AFTER THE OTHER INTONE "COME IN WITH THE DUTCHMAN"

Yo-Yo Gun:
"COME IN WITH THE DUTCHMAN"

169
EXTERIOR. STREETS. TWILIGHT. MEDIUM SHOTS.

The yo-yo jumps up into the yo-yo gun's fist, and the fist flashes forward, breaking a nose. The Chinese gun beats a runner up with karate. Others are worked over with broken bottles and blackjacks and bicycle chains.

170
INTERIOR. BASEMENT CABARET. NIGHT. MEDIUM SHOT.

Harlem underground cabaret: pot smoking, drinking; fags, pimps, whores, dope peddlers, runners, some tourists from downtown. A white faggot in sharp runner drag prances on-stage.

Artist:
Come in with the Dutchman.
Come in with the Dutchman.
Come in with the Dutchman.
Or else!

He does a split prat fall, clutching his chest.

Come in with the Dutchman.
Come in with the Dutchman.
Come in with the Dutchman.
Or else!

He smashes a bag of ketchup against his face, grabs his crotch and falls forward wiggling his ass obscenely.

APPLAUSE

171
DUTCH'S PICTURE FILLS SCREEN. NEWSPAPER HEADLINES APPEAR.

DUTCH SCHULTZ INDICTED FOR INCOME TAX EVASION

APPLAUSE CONTINUES THROUGH THIS TAKE

172
INTERIOR. CAR. EVENING. MEDIUM SHOT.

Bo Weinberg at the wheel, Dixie Davis in front seat, Martin Krompier and Jules Martin in the back seat. Car weaves through midtown traffic.

Federal Income

PLEASE CLASSIFY AND FILE WITH FIN(

FLEGENHEIMER

RIGHT HAN(

LEFT HAND

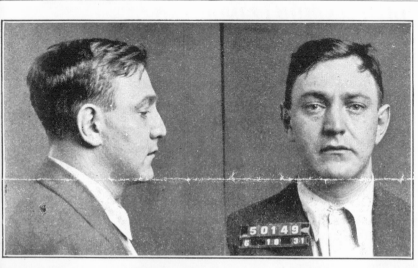

ARTHUR FLEGENHEIMER, aliases DUTCH SCHULTZ

ARTHUR SCHULTZ, GEORGE SCHULTZ, JOSEPH HARMON
AND CHARLES HARMON.

DESCRIPTION—Age 34 years; height 5 feet, 7 inches;
weight 165 pounds; medium build; brown hair; gray eyes;

Bo Weinberg is a magical driver. Traffic opens for him like the Red Sea and closes behind him.

TRAFFIC

Bo runs a red light and turns wrong way down a one-way street. Dixie Davis clutches his briefcase nervously. Bo glances in car mirror.

Bo Weinberg:
Lost them.

Sudden darkness indicates lapse of time. The car is driving through an area of deserted warehouses, vacant lots, and cobblestone streets. Car pulls into garage of apartment building.

TRAFFIC SOUND FADES INTO THE DISTANCE

CRICKETS AND CROAKING FROGS

173
INTERIOR. HALL. NIGHT. MEDIUM SHOT.

Bo Weinberg rings bell. The door is opened by Lulu Rosencrantz. They nod coldly. Behind Lulu is a hall and another door.

174
INTERIOR. APARTMENT LIVING ROOM. NIGHT. MEDIUM SHOT.

Living room like the show window of a furniture store: glass-fronted bookcases, furniture upholstered in striped red-and-white satins, wallpaper to match, shaded desk lamps, a fireplace with gas logs, small bronze statue of Rodin's *The Thinker* on the scrolled marble mantelpiece. Above that, Aurora ushers in the horses of Apollo. Lulu Rosencrantz, Dutch, and Abe Landau have been playing pinochle; board, cards, beer glasses on table. Dutch shakes hands with Dixie and Martin Krompier and Bo Weinberg.

GREETINGS

ACTION | SOUND

Martin Krompier:
Arthur, this is Jules Martin. He handles dissemination and collection for Union 16.

Dutch:
Glad to know you, Martin.

Jules Martin:
Glad to know you, Mr Flegenheimer. Nice place you got here.

175
INTERIOR. HOSPITAL ROOM. NIGHT. MEDIUM SHOT.

HOSPITAL SOUND EFFECTS

Dutch:
Shut up you gotta big mouth . . . I can't tell you to. That is not what you have in the book.

Police stenographer writes this down.

176
INTERIOR. APARTMENT LIVING ROOM. NIGHT. MEDIUM SHOT.

Dixie Davis:
I've been down to Washington again, Arthur, and it's still no deal. They say you have to surrender and stand trial.

Dutch:
A quarter million isn't too much for the man who can deliver.

Dixie Davis:
Federal case, Arthur. It's tough to fix. Those boys don't shake hands.

Dutch:
Well, keep on it . . . Let's go to the office.

177
INTERIOR. OFFICE ROOM. NIGHT. MEDIUM SHOT.

Apartment room turned into office . . . desk, adding machine, filing cabinets, map of New York on the wall. Dixie Davis looks uneasily at the filing cabinets.

Dixie Davis:
What's in there, Arthur?

Dutch:
Don't worry about it Dixie. I flick this switch (*he touches a switch under a corner of the desk*) and that cabinet turns into an electric toaster.

Martin Krompier:
Here are some standouts, Dutch.

He hands Dutch several cards.

178

INTERIOR. NIGHT SPOT. NIGHT. MEDIUM SHOT.

Voice of Dutch off-screen:
The Silver Cord.

The proprietor is unhooking the famous silver cord to admit favored clients to the Inner Room. Some clients he bows in, stepping back with the coiled rope in his arms. Others are barely given room to squeeze through.

Mr Unsuitable and party present themselves at the rope. There is something *wrong* about him, and he knows it. He has a hangdog look, and his hands tremble.

Mr Unsuitable:
But I have a reservation.

Proprietor:
Sorry, there doesn't seem to be a table reserved in your name.

179

INTERIOR. HOSPITAL ROOM. NIGHT. MEDIUM SHOT.

There is only one detective in the room. He is dozing in a chair.

HOSPITAL SOUND EFFECTS

Voice of Albert Stern:
Please let me get in and eat.

Police stenographer writes this down. The detective wakes up.

Detective:
Who shot you?

Voice of Dutch:
The boss himself.

180

INTERIOR. SILVER CORD. NIGHT. MEDIUM SHOT.

Albert Stern in a filthy evening jacket pocked with cigarette burns, his pants held up by a length of rope,

runs toward the silver cord, the doorman ten feet behind him. Behind the doorman is a flying wedge of panhandlers. They burst through the cord, ripping it from the hook.

181
INTERIOR. INNER ROOM. NIGHT. MEDIUM SHOT.

The panhandlers invade the dining room. They seep in from the kitchen and the fire exits. The waiters try to oust them but they are like sacks of mendicant concrete, clutching at the guests with filthy fingers, snatching food and drinks from the tables, urinating on the floor, sitting down with the guests.

Albert Stern:
Just let me taste your drink. Mind if I sit down, Governor?

182
INTERIOR. DUTCH'S OFFICE. DAY. MEDIUM SHOT.

Dutch, Bo Weinberg, George Weinberg, Lulu Rosencrantz. George Weinberg hands Dutch an account sheet. Dutch looks through it, frowning.

Dutch:
Not so good.

George Weinberg:
It's like booking the bangtails, Dutch. Sometimes you get hit, but it evens out.

Dutch:
Everybody jumps on one number, we got no way to lay off the play . . . Now suppose we shift from treasury reports to pari-mutuel figures? . . . A big bet just under the bell could change the last two numbers.

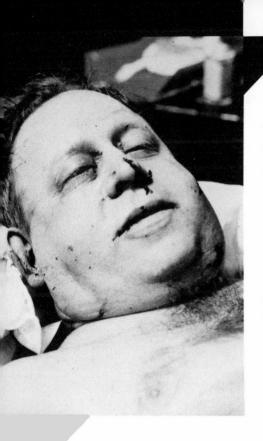

George Weinberg:
An adding machine couldn't do it, Dutch.

Dutch:
How about a *human* adding machine?

George Weinberg:
You mean Aba Daba Berman?

Dutch:
That's my boy.

George Weinberg:
He's expensive, Dutch. Best lay-off man in the business.

183
INTERIOR. DINING ROOM. NIGHT. MEDIUM SHOT.

A flashy, over-expensive spot. Officious waiters with an exaggerated flourish deposit dishes with silver covers on tables.

He lifts the cover to reveal the bloated corpse of a huge rat swimming in axle grease and garnished with garbage.

He lifts cover to reveal a buzzard cooked in sewage.

He lifts cover to reveal a live horseshoe crab on its back in used condoms, shit-stained newspapers, and bloody Kotex.
The guests scream, gag, cover their faces with napkins.

Voice of Dutch off-screen:
Chez Victor.

Waiter 1:
Voilà le *Lapin Chasseur.*

Waiter 2:
Voilà le *Faisan Suprême.*

Waiter 3:
Voilà les *Fruits de Mer.*

184
INTERIOR. PHONE BOOTH. DAY. MEDIUM SHOT.

Aba Daba Berman in phone booth, the phone cradled, watches the tote board. The bell rings once. He puts down phone and scuttles to the ticket window. Just as the bell rings for the last time he slides five thousand-dollar bills through the window.

Aba Daba Berman:
Earl King to win.

Horses leap from starting gate.

THEY'RE OFF!

185
EXTERIOR. NIGHTCLUB ENTRANCE. NIGHT. MEDIUM SHOT.

Dutch's voice off-screen:
The 400.

Chauffeur-driven limousines, guests in evening dress bowed in by obsequious doorman. Suddenly a truck stops and a pack of screaming faggots leap out. They buzz by the doorman like hornets.

186
INTERIOR. CLUB 400. NIGHT. MEDIUM SHOT.

They fill the club screeching and camping. They snatch tablecloths, curtains, and drapes and do impersonation acts.

187
INTERIOR. OFFICE. DAY. MEDIUM SHOT.

Dutch, Bo and George, Lulu Rosencrantz.

Dutch:
There's still too much overhead. For one thing, the runners are overpaid.

They now have full protection thanks to my organization. I'm cutting their percentage from 33 to 25.

Bo Weinberg:
They won't stand still for it, Dutch.

Lulu Rosencrantz:
They will if Dutch says so.

Bo gives him a sour look.

188
INTERIOR. HALL. DAY. MEDIUM SHOT.

Hall where the 2,000 striking runners have assembled. Speaker on platform raises his hands.

MUSICAL SCORE OF JOE HILL

MUSIC STOPS

Speaker:
We all know why we are assembled in this hall tonight. And I think most of us know that some workers are not here because of intimidation and threats directed against them and against their families . . . Well, I'm here to tell you that if we stand firmly together, no threats and no intimidation can prevail.

CHEERS FROM THE AUDIENCE

If we allow ourselves to be browbeaten and intimidated, where will it end? . . . 25 percent? 20 percent? 15 percent?

189
INTERIOR. HOSPITAL ROOM. DAY. MEDIUM SHOT.

HOSPITAL SOUND EFFECTS

Voice of Dutch:
Communistic strike . . . baloney . . . honestly, this is a habit I get.

2nd detective comes in with coffee and sandwiches. Police stenographer

ACTION	SOUND

writes down what Dutch has said.

Sometimes I give it and sometimes I don't . . .

2nd Detective:
Baloney is right.

190

INTERIOR. HALL. DAY. MEDIUM SHOT.

HOSPITAL SOUND EFFECTS CARRY OVER FOR A FEW SECONDS

Speaker:
Now, D. S. Flegenheimer tells us we are fully protected legally, financially, and personally by his organization. He tells us there are no risks left. Well, I'd like to ask how many people in this hall have been in jail in the past week?

CHORUS OF ME ME ME

And I'd like to ask how many people in this hall have paid off a bet out of their own pocket because somebody on the other end of the line made a mistake when you phoned in a number?

191

INTERIOR. HOSPITAL ROOM. DAY. MEDIUM SHOT.

The detectives are eating sandwiches.

Voice of Dutch:
You get ahead with the dot dash system . . . didn't I speak that time last night? Whose number is that in your pocketbook, Phil? 13780?

Stenographer writes this down.

192
INTERIOR. HALL. DAY. MEDIUM SHOT.

HOSPITAL SOUND EFFECTS CARRY OVER
A FEW SECONDS

Speaker turns his face to the light to show a scar running from temple to chin.

Speaker:
Shoemaker's knife . . . used to cut leather . . . It cuts other things, too. 32-20 . . . It went straight through. I was lucky. Some other workers haven't been that lucky . . . And then D.S. Flegenheimer goes down to the stale flower market and sends along some wilted petunias to the next of kin . . . How many of you in this hall have scars like these received in the service of D. S. Flegenheimer?

He pulls open his shirt to show a bullet scar.

Members of the audience pull open shirts, drop pants, part hair, open mouths.

SHOTGUN
BASEBALL BAT
BROKEN BOTTLE
ROLL OF NICKELS

The time to make a stand is right here and right now. 33 percent or *walk out*. And that doesn't mean 32 percent.

They wave placards . . .
"33 PERCENT OR WALK OUT"

CHEERS FROM THE AUDIENCE

193
INTERIOR. OFFICE. DAY. MEDIUM SHOT.

Dutch, Bo Weinberg, Dixie Davis in hide-out apartment.

Bo Weinberg:
They been out on strike a week now, Dutch. With no money coming in to meet payrolls, we could lose the whole territory.

Dutch:
Stabbing me in the back when I'm pinned down here . . . All right,

Dutch reaches for his lumpy overcoat and puts it on.	back to work at 33 percent . . . Come on, Dixie.
	Bo Weinberg: Where are you going, Dutch?

194

NEWSPAPER HEADLINES AND PICTURE . . .

DUTCH SCHULTZ SURRENDERS...
TO STAND TRIAL...
DUTCH SCHULTZ RELEASED ON $75,000 BAIL

Chorus of Underworld Voices:
The Dutchman is going away . . .
Five years at least . . .
He won't come back . . .
The Dutchman is through . . .

195

INTERIOR. OFFICE. DAY. MEDIUM SHOT.

This is Dutch's business office which suggests a hotel lobby. Dutch, Bo Weinberg, George Weinberg, Lulu Rosencrantz, Dixie Davis. Dixie Davis is a fast talker and a fast thinker. Vain, cowardly, treacherous, he manages to be likable. He has a way of smiling when he relates bad news.	*Dixie Davis:* We can't beat this case on the evidence, Arthur . . . We have to make a direct appeal to public opinion. First step is a change of venue . . . upstate some place . . . Those farmers don't like paying income tax any more than you do. And find a local lawyer, the right local lawyer. Out-of-town lawyers are murder in

a local scene like this. I'll be there in an advisory capacity, of course. Next step is build up your public image . . . convince every hick on that jury before he sits on that jury that you are a nice guy, just like he is, having a little trouble with the revenuers . . .

196
INTERIOR. OFFICE. DAY. MEDIUM SHOT.

Close up of DUNCAN & BRADSHAW PUBLIC RELATIONS COUNSELORS. Dissolves to luxurious office. There is a Modigliani on the wall. Behind the desk is a white-haired man with soft, beautiful manicured hands. As he talks he punctuates his words with long pauses, during which his eyes mist over dreamily.

Mr Bradshaw:
Well, Mr Flegenheimer, we need a peg to hang it on. (*Pause.*) Something that will take hold. (*Pause.*) Something that people will associate with your name. (*Long dreamy pause.*) How about this? . . . Arthur Flegenheimer, the man who collects rare books?

Dutch:
Arthur Flegenheimer, the man who collects rare books.

197
EXTERIOR. STREET. DAY. MEDIUM SHOT.

Dutch, Dixie Davis, Bo and George Weinberg, Lulu Rosencrantz.

Dutch:
Call in the Whisperer.

George Weinberg:
He's on carny tour, Dutch.

Lulu Rosencrantz:
I know where to find him.

HOSPITAL SOUND EFFECTS MIX BRIEFLY
WITH STREET SOUNDS

198
INTERIOR. DUTCH'S OFFICE. DAY. MEDIUM SHOT.

Dutch is seated at the desk with a drink. The Whisperer sits in a straight-backed chair looking like a grey, anonymous corpse. George and Bo Weinberg, Dixie Davis, and Lulu Rosencrantz.

Dutch:
O.K. Whisperer. Here are your lines . . . Arthur Flegenheimer, the man who collects rare books . . .

The Whisperer (speaks without moving his lips; this is done with tape recorders): Arthur Flegenheimer, the man who collects rare books.
(It is a perfect imitation of Dutch's voice. It is at the same time a sticky sound that catches and stirs in the throat.)

Dixie Davis clutches his throat uneasily.

The Whisperer repeats the same phrase backward.

Dutch:
Whazat he's saying?

George Weinberg:
He's saying it backward, Dutch. It acts on the subconscious.

Dutch:
Oh you mean like doubletalk.

George Weinberg:
Yeah, that's it. He can say it fast or slow or mix it around . . .

The Whisperer demonstrates variations.

Dutch:
Arthur   Flegenheimer   generous
friendly.

The Whisperer:
Arthur   Flegenheimer   generous
friendly.

Dutch:
The Dutchman's trouble could be
yours or mine.

199
INTERIOR. RANCH OFFICE. DAY. MEDIUM SHOT.

Rancher sits in battered swivel chair. An Inland Revenue agent paces up and down.

COWS BELLOW OFF-SCREEN. THE WHISPERER REPEATS: "THE DUTCHMAN'S TROUBLE COULD BE YOURS OR MINE"

Rancher:
You want to count my cows Mister?

Agent:
No, Mr Peterson, I don't want to count your cows. I want to see your books.

Rancher:
I don't keep books, Mister.

Agent:
Well, Mister, I'm here to tell you you owe the United States government $16,623 in back taxes.

BELLOWING OF CATTLE REACHES A CRESCENDO AS THE WHISPERER BOOMS OUT "THE DUTCHMAN'S TROUBLE COULD BE YOURS OR MINE"

ACTION	SOUND

200

INTERIOR. OFFICE. DAY. MEDIUM SHOT.

Dutch:
Experts from Washington telling us
what to plant.

The Whisperer:
Experts from Washington telling us
what to plant.

201

INTERIOR. GOVERNMENT OFFICE. DAY. MEDIUM SHOT.

This is office of the Bureau of Agri-
culture. Sullen farmers look at
forms. A bureaucrat sits at a table
behind a pile of forms.

THE WHISPERER'S VOICE CARRIES
THROUGH THIS SCENE

*Bureaucrat (he talks in a weary
nasal whine):*
It's all explained in the forms. . .
⅔ of present acreage is the quota
on any crops specified in section 13D
unless exempted under section
C . . .

202

INTERIOR. OFFICE. DAY. MEDIUM SHOT.

Dutch:
So he sold beer? What's wrong about
that?

203

EXTERIOR. RURAL STILL. NIGHT. MEDIUM SHOT.

THE WHISPERER REPEATS OFF-SCREEN
"SO HE SOLD BEER? WHAT'S WRONG
ABOUT THAT?"

Peter and Vincent Coll dressed as
hillbillies lounge by a still, rifles
propped against a tree.

FROGS AND CRICKETS

204
INTERIOR. OFFICE. DAY. MEDIUM SHOT.

Lulu Rosencrantz takes out a deputy's badge and pins it to his vest.

Dutch:
Now we're all going on tour.

Bo Weinberg:
What's *that?*

Lulu Rosencrantz:
It's my badge. I been deputized.

HOSPITAL SOUND EFFECTS

205
INTERIOR. TOWN LIBRARY. DAY. MEDIUM SHOT.

An open bookcase with rare books bears the label "Donated By Arthur Flegenheimer." Dutch, Lulu, Dixie Davis, reporters, librarian, local Chamber of Commerce on set. Among the photographers is the Whisperer.

Librarian:
Oh, Mr Flegenheimer they're beautiful.

Chamber of Commerce Representative:
On behalf of the city of Malone I want to thank you, Mr Flegenheimer.

Dutch shakes hands. The Whisperer takes his picture.

VOICE OF THE WHISPERER ADJUSTED TO SOUND LEVEL OF VOICES IN THE ROOM SO THAT IT IS BARELY AUDIBLE "ARTHUR FLEGENHEIMER, THE MAN WHO COLLECTS RARE BOOKS . . . ARTHUR FLEGENHEIMER GENEROUS FRIENDLY . . ."

206
EXTERIOR. STOCK FAIR. DAY. MEDIUM SHOT.

Dutch flanked by Lulu and Dixie mingles with the crowd. Turkeys, hams bear the label "Donated by Arthur Flegenheimer."
Dutch nods and smiles . . . He stops to pet a prize bull. "Cup donated by Arthur Flegenheimer" . . . "Beer keg donated by Arthur Flegenheimer" . . .
Glasses are filled and drained . . .
The sky clouds over.

COWS, PIGS, CHICKENS

VOICE OF THE WHISPERER "ARTHUR FLEGENHEIMER GENEROUS, FRIENDLY . . . THE DUTCHMAN'S TROUBLE COULD BE YOURS OR MINE. SO HE SOLD BEER? WHAT'S WRONG ABOUT THAT? THE DUTCHMAN'S TROUBLE COULD BE YOURS OR MINE"

Dutch:
I need a drink. Let's get out of here.

207
POSTCARD SHOT OF THE OLD HARMONY HOTEL. WINTER SCENE.

Dutch's voice off-screen:
I don't want harmony . . . I want harmony . . .

HOSPITAL SOUND EFFECTS

208
INTERIOR. HOTEL ROOM. NIGHT. MEDIUM SHOT.

Room in the Old Harmony Hotel . . . Red curtains and carpet turn-of-the-century decor. *The Death of Stonewall Jackson* on the wall. Dixie Davis is reading *Collier's* magazine. Martin Krompier looks at the ceiling. They are both very bored with the argument between Dutch and Jules Martin that has obviously been going on for some time. They think it is a long, loud-mouthed argument that will get nowhere. Jules Martin is under a similar misapprehension. Dutch pours a drink. He shoves his face within inches of Martin's.

Dutch:
So Jules Judas Martin thought the Dutchman was through didn't he? Thought you could put your big greasy mitt in for forty thousand clams, didn't you?

Jules Martin:
Look, Dutch, we don't owe a nickel.

Dutch:
Cut that out we don't owe a nickel.

HOSPITAL SOUND EFFECTS

Jules Martin (he opens his mouth to say "Say, listen . . ." he gets out): "Say, list . . ."

Dutch:
Shut up you gotta big mouth.

As he says this Dutch flips a snub nosed .38 from an inside holster in his waistband, shoves it right in Jules's mouth and pulls the trigger. Jules falls to the floor screaming, moaning, spitting blood and smoke. Dixie Davis jumps up and the magazine falls to the floor at his feet. Martin Krompier is on his feet, no less appalled by Dutch's insane act. Ashen, Dixie opens a door into adjoining room and goes through, followed by Krompier.

MUFFLED MEATY SOUND
HOSPITAL SOUND EFFECTS CONTINUE

209
INTERIOR. ADJOINING HOTEL ROOM. NIGHT. MEDIUM SHOT.

MOANS AND SCREAMS OF JULES MARTIN CONTINUE THROUGHOUT THIS SCENE

Lulu Rosencrantz is tilted back in a chair, his deputy badge showing.

Lulu Rosencrantz (phlegmatically): What happened?

Martin Krompier:
Dutch is crazy. He just shot a man for nothing.

ACTION	SOUND

Dutch comes in, putting away his pistol. He looks worried. Lulu comes down on his feet, walks across the room, mixes a drink, and hands it to Dutch, who takes a long gulp. He turns to Dixie Davis.
Dixie Davis snatches up his coat, hat, and briefcase.

Dutch:
Give me a drink Lulu.

You must hate me for this, Dick.

Dixie Davis:
To do a thing like that right in front of me, Arthur . . . After all, I'm a professional man.

Dutch:
Lulu, you'd better go in the lobby and get that clerk out of the way so he won't see Dick walk out.

Lulu goes out. Dixie Davis puts his coat on. He steps out and freezes in the doorway.

210
INTERIOR. HALL. NIGHT. TRACKING SHOT.

Dixie Davis in doorway. Hotel porter carrying a bucket over one arm walks by, whistling "Home Sweet Home" down the empty corridor.

211
INTERIOR. HOSPITAL ROOM. NIGHT. MEDIUM SHOT.

Doctor is filing the end off an ampoule of morphine and filling the syringe.

1st Detective:
Can't you give him something that will get him to talk, Doctor?

Doctor:
Talk to who? The man is delirious.

Voice of Dutch:
Oh, and then he clips me. Come on, cut that out we don't owe a nickel . . . "Say list . . ."

Flash of Jules Martin arguing.

1st Detective:
Control yourself.

212
INTERIOR. OFFICE. DAY. MEDIUM SHOT.

Office of the DA. Newspaper on desk with headlines:
DUTCH SCHULTZ ACQUITTED
ON TAX CHARGES.
The DA's mustache bristles with indignation. He presses intercom button.

District Attorney:
Send in Coyne and Ahearn.

The two investigators stand in front of the desk.

I want to you to drop everything else and concentrate on the Dutchman . . . Keep digging . . .

213
EXTERIOR. STREETS. DAY. MEDIUM SHOTS.

Same Harlem sets as were used in sequence showing Dutch's takeover of Harlem. The two agents are showing Dutch's picture, taking state-

ments, writing down figures. Cut-in with these shots are pictures of Dewey . . . Newspaper pictures, bigger and bigger until campaign posters fill the screen.

214
EXTERIOR. NEWARK REMOVALS AND STORAGE. NIGHT. MEDIUM SHOT.

Cobblestone streets, weeds growing through.

FROGS AND CRICKETS

215
INTERIOR. OFFICE. NIGHT. MEDIUM SHOT.

The office is sparsely furnished—a desk, a small Burroughs adding machine, chairs, a rusty filing cabinet.

ACTION	SOUND

Room should convey look of having been closed for years, and the windows are boarded over. Dutch paces up and down. Also on set are Dixie Davis, Bo Weinberg, Lulu Rosencrantz, and Abe Landau.

Dutch:
Run out of New York by a snot-nosed DA . . . Washed up in Jersey. What are you doing about this, Dick?

Dixie Davis (he spreads his hands and smiles):
Nothing, Arthur. I can't reach him. Nobody can.

Dutch:
Nobody? And what is the *Board* going to do about this, Bo? What is the big Board going to do?

Bo Weinberg:
I don't know, Dutch.

Dutch:
Don't you? I thought you had an inside line.

Bo Weinberg:
I know they want to talk about it. You can sit in.

Dutch:
Can you fix that, Bo? Can you fix it with their serene highnesses, the acid-throwing wops?

Bo Weinberg:
What's eating you, Dutch? Of course you have the right to sit in as an interested party.

Dutch:
What's eating all of us? The *Board* . . . And who runs the Board? The wops run it.

Bo Weinberg:
You can't buck them, Dutch.

Dutch:
Can't I? I've got a hundred loyal guns . . . If I can just get this DA this . . . What's the word, Dick?

Dixie Davis:
Nemesis, Arthur.

Dutch:
This *nemesis* off my back.

216
INTERIOR. BOARDROOM. DAY OR NIGHT UNCERTAIN. MEDIUM SHOT.

Campaign poster of the DA dissolves to twelve men seated at long table. The cameras (two) that cover this table do not move or pan from face to face. The actors call attention to themselves by what they say. Background shots vaguely seen are taken from other sets in the film. This is the hospital room, Dutch's office, the Palace Chop House. At one end of the table sits an old Mafia brother with dark glasses. At the other end sits Lepke Buchalter the Judge, doe-eyed and enigmatic. He is the nominal chairman but the old man is obviously in control. On the old man's left sit Dutch and Bo Weinberg. On his right is Anastasia. On Lepke's right is Lucky Luciano, on his left is Gurrah, his snarling partner.

Old Man:
Kick him upstairs into a governor.

Albert Anastasia:
Or president even . . .

Member 3:
DAs come and go.

Member 4:
Why wait? I say hit him.

Member 5:
We can ride this out. I say forget him.

Gurrah:
Hit.

Lucky Luciano:
This is 1935, not 1925 . . . Time to pack in the cowboy act.

Member 8:
Undecided.

Member 9:
I'd have to think about it.

Dutch:
I say he's got to be hit on the head. We gotta make an example.

Lepke Buchalter:
An example of what, Mr Flegenheimer? There seems to be a difference of opinion here. I think we are all agreed that this is an important decision. *Very important.* I suggest we adjourn until next Tuesday. That will give those of you who are undecided time to make up your minds.

Dutch:
But suppose next week we vote to take him? We should have the job staked out and ready to go.

Lepke Buchalter:
That makes sense. Albert, will you check this out.

Albert Anastasia:
Sure. Ready to go next week if that's the way you all want it . . .

217
EXTERIOR. STREET. DAY. MEDIUM SHOT.

Street scene similar to the scene in which the Coll brothers attempt to kill Rao. Children playing, women with baby carriages. Anastasia in there pushing a borrowed child around on a tricycle. He is a thin, very ugly Italian, with a big nose and a charming smile. The DA emerges from an apartment entrance flanked by two bodyguards. He nods quietly to a few acquaintances.

District Attorney:
This is a great country . . . those people back there . . . It's our job to see that people like that are protected.

Bodyguard (indifferently stifling a yawn):
Yes sir.

The DA is walking toward corner drugstore. Pushing his child on tricycle, the stake-out man follows. The DA enters a drugstore. The two guards stand at the door. The stake-out man is now in front of the drugstore. Stake-out man tosses a sharp glance into the drugstore. The DA is in the phone booth. At the counter, the druggist is talking to a shabby customer. The druggist holds a piece of paper in his hand.

Child:
I want an ice-cream cone, Daddy.

218
INTERIOR. DRUGSTORE. DAY. MEDIUM SHOT.

Camera zooms in for a quick close-up of the Rx the druggist is holding. It is Rx for twenty ¼ grain tables of morphine sulphate. The druggist looks across his bifocals at the emaciated face of Albert Stern.

Albert Stern:
It's a legitimate prescription.

| ACTION | SOUND |

Druggist:
Maybe. But don't be coming in here
with your prescriptions every Tuesday and Thursday.

The DA is talking in the phone
booth.

219
INTERIOR. HOSPITAL ROOM. DAY. MEDIUM SHOT.

Voice of Dutch off-screen:
Let him harness himself to you and
then bother you. You can play jacks
and girls do that with a soft ball.

The stenographer writes this down.
The two detectives look at each
other in disgust.

1st Detective:
Now what are we sitting here for?

220
INTERIOR. BOARDROOM. DAY. MEDIUM SHOT.

Same seating arrangement and
actors as before.

Albert Anastasia:
Every morning at 8:40 he leaves the
apartment and goes to a drugstore
on the corner of 79th and 3rd and
makes a phone call.

221
INTERIOR. DRUGSTORE. DAY. MEDIUM SHOT.

Man is talking to druggist.

Gun:
Yeah . . . That one with the wild
cherry in it . . . (*He points to a
shelf of cough syrups.*)

DA enters and goes in phone booth.
Druggist hands man his purchase.
The man draws automatic with
silencer and shoots druggist twice
in chest. Druggist sags behind the
counter. Man walks over to phone
booth and pulls it open with one
hand. He puts four bullets in the
DAs back. He walks out past the

guards whistling, turns corner and gets in car. Briefly glimpsed the man is Charlie Workman. As the car drives away, we glimpse the snarling Coll brothers from the Rao scene.

222
INTERIOR. BOARDROOM. DAY. MEDIUM SHOT.

Dutch:
It's perfect. The phone booth is a natural.

Member 9:
Plenty could go wrong . . . the druggist knocks something over . . .

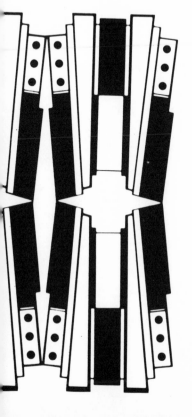

Member 5:
The DA lets out a squawk . . .
People squawk with bullets in them
. . .

Gurrah:
Hit the two schmuckles on the door
. . .

Lepke Buchalter:
Let's decide whether we are going
to hit or not before going into these
details.

Member 4:
We're doing all right. Why stick the
neck out?

Member 8:
The Federals will jump on the
rackets . . . We'll be chased out of
the country.

Lucky Luciano:
You have to take a broad general
view of things. It's not good business.

Member 9:
A hundred loud-mouthed DAs
would spring from his coffin.

Lepke Buchalter:
We'll put it to a vote. For or against?

Old Man:
Against.

*Albert Anastasia (he lifts his hands
and turns them out):*
. . . It's beautiful . . . but . . . (*he
drops his hands palm down on the
table*) against.

Member 3:
Against.

Member 4:
Times have changed. I'm against it.

Gurrah:
For.

Lepke Buchalter:
Aroused   public   opinion . . . bad
press . . . bad   business . . . my
vote is against.

Lucky Luciano:
Against.

Member 8:
Against.

Member 9:
I'm against it.

Dutch:
Wait a minute here . . .

Dutch stands up.

Lepke Buchalter:
You are outvoted, Mr Flegenheimer.

Dutch:
I still say he's gotta be hit and he's
gonna be hit . . .

DEAD SILENCE IN THE BOARDROOM

HOSPITAL SOUND EFFECTS

Voice off-screen:
The doctor wants you to lie quiet.

223
EXTERIOR. CAR. NIGHT. MEDIUM SHOT.

Car entering Holland Tunnel. Piggy is at the wheel. The hulking snarling strangler Mendy Weiss sits on the jump seat. In the back seat are Charlie Workman and Jimmy the Shrew. Workman is a cool, casual killer, dressed in a tailor-made twilight blue suit and grey fedora . . . pale face, cold metallic grey eyes. The Shrew is dressed in a tight pea-green suit and grey fedora . . . smooth poreless red skin tight over the cheek bones, lips parted from long yellow teeth the color of old ivory. The tunnel light rings their heads with an orange halo.

NEWS AND WEATHER ON CAR RADIO

224
INTERIOR. BACK ROOM OF PALACE CHOP HOUSE. NIGHT. MEDIUM SHOT.

Dutch is sitting at a table with Lulu Rosencrantz, Abe Landau and Otto Daba Berman. Beer mugs on the table, a cigar smoking in an ash tray. Aba Daba is working an adding machine and writing figures down on ledger paper. Chinese cook appears in upper panel of a green door. The cook nods and disappears. Aba Daba Berman passes an account sheet to Dutch. Dutch studies it and smiles. Close-up shows account sheet.

Dutch:
Hey, Wong.
A steak medium rare, with french fries.

Dutch:
Gross for past seven weeks 827,253 net 148,369 . . . Well, we're still in business . . . (*he stands up.*) I gotta call from nature. Right back.

SOUND OF FRYING FROM THE KITCHEN

HOSPITAL SOUND EFFECTS

Voice of Dutch off-screen:
Come on open the soap duckets.

99

225
EXTERIOR. FRONT OF PALACE CHOP HOUSE. NIGHT. MEDIUM SHOT.

This is a grey, ghostly scene. Death car draws up in front of the Palace Chop House. Workman, the Shrew, and Mendy Weiss get out. Workman looks up and down the street. A few anonymous grey pedestrians walking by. The three killers slide through the front door.

Voice of Dutch off-screen:
I don't know who can have done it . . . anybody.

| ACTION | SOUND |

INTERIOR. PALACE CHOP HOUSE. NIGHT. MEDIUM SHOT.

Mendy Weiss pulls a sawed-off pump shotgun out from under his coat. Bartender disappears behind bar. Workman jerks his thumb at the shotgun.

Workman:
Save that. We may need it on the way out.

Workman and the Shrew walk down the bar unhurried, but wasting no time. Workman's coat is open and there are two .38 Smith & Wesson revolvers in his belt. When he reaches the men's room he slips another revolver from his hip pocket. This is a sawed-off Smith & Wesson .45 revolver. He opens the door, sees someone washing his hands. He fires with the .45. The cartridge spits and the flying fragments spatter his pale face with blood. (At this point film switches to color.) His expression does not change. He tosses the .45 into a towel basket. He covers the few steps to the door of the back room, the Shrew at his side. The three men in the back room dive for their guns. Grabbing his wrist with the left hand the Shrew shoots Aba Daba Berman through the head. A computer screen explodes and goes out on screen. Workman, with his gloved left hand, steadies the heavy revolver, holding it on each side of the cylinder as he methodically pours bullets into Landau and Rosencrantz. He drops his empty revolver on the floor. Shooting stops.

GUN SHOT

PISTOL SHOTS

HOSPITAL SOUND EFFECTS
BABBLE OF DUTCH'S LAST WORDS BE-HIND GUN SHOTS

AS SHOOTING STOPS HOSPITAL SOUND EFFECTS ARE AUDIBLE AND CARRY OVER INTO NEXT SCENE

227
INTERIOR. OPERATING ROOM. NIGHT. MEDIUM SHOT.

Ether vertigo in this scene is indicated by taking shots from body interior . . . gullet, lungs, liver . . . and rotating . . . Brief flash of Dutch on the operating table. Doctor peeling off gloves.

Doctor's Voice:
That liver just isn't going to make it . . . Sew him up . . . patch him up . . . quarter grain MS every four hours as long as he lasts.

228
INTERIOR. HOSPITAL ROOM. NIGHT. MEDIUM SHOT.

Nurse with a hypo on a tray elbows her way through a room full of reporters and detectives. She gives Dutch a shot. Reporters and detectives seen from the bed. One of the detectives carries a paper with front-page headlines.

Dutch:
Has it been in any of the other papers?

229
INTERIOR. OFFICE OF POLICE COMMISSIONER. DAY. MEDIUM SHOT.

Press conference. The police commisioner behind his desk.

Reporter:
Any line on the Dutch Schultz shoot down, Commissioner?

Commissioner:
We have. One of the gunmen has positively been identified as Albert Stern.

Reporter:
Who's this Albert Stern?

Commissioner:
Because of his spectacles and his mild appearance he is known as the Teacher. Wild Boy would be a better name for him. A hophead gunman, top trigger for the Big Six

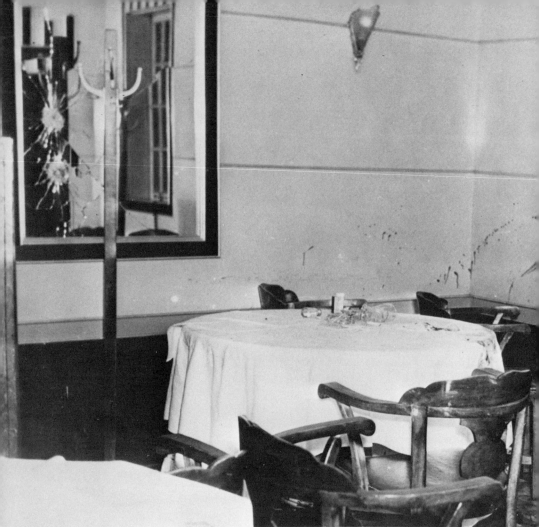

Syndicate, he is probably one of the most dangerous killers alive today.

230
INTERIOR. POOLROOM. NIGHT. MEDIUM SHOT.

Ghostly shot. Pool players. Dressed in his filthy dinner jacket, his pants held up by a length of rope, Albert Stern sits on a bench watching the

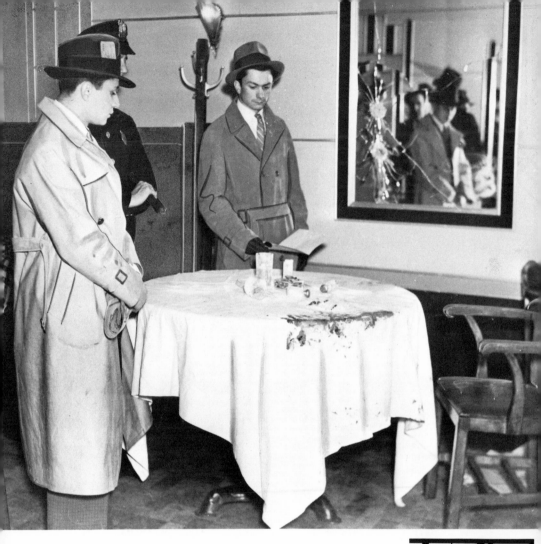

game. With a sudden galvanized movement he stands up and pulls a .32 single-action Smith & Wesson revolver from his coat pocket. The gun is nickle plated and pocked with rust. Verdigris from the cartridges has stained the cylinder. It looks like something that has been in a drawer for thirty years. Slowly the players raise their hands. A player tosses two dollars onto the table. Albert Stern snatches the money and rushes out.

Albert Stern:
All I want is two dollars.

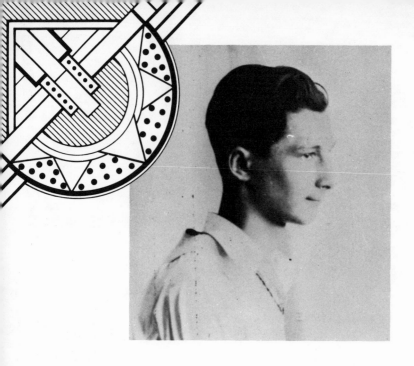

The players go on with the game.

Player:
There it is, kid.

2nd Player:
Hey George, bring those beers, will you?

231
INTERIOR. TENEMENT APARTMENT. NIGHT. MEDIUM SHOT.

Albert Stern opens door and stands against it, getting his breath. With trembling hands, he opens a packet of heroin and takes a shot. He puts the eye dropper down. The walls are covered with newspaper pictures of Dutch Schultz.

HOSPITAL SOUND EFFECTS

232
INTERIOR. HOSPITAL ROOM. NIGHT. MEDIUM SHOT.

In this shot, scenes from Dutch's delirium are cut-in with the hospital room at rapid intervals. Dutch stag-

gers out of the Palace Chop House
lavatory clutching his bleeding side.
Cut back to Dutch in hospital room.

Dutch:
Oh mama mama mama I been shot
through the liver.

Detective:
The doctor wants you to lie quiet.

Maternity scene.

Dutch:
Mama don't tear don't rip . . .

CRY OF NEWBORN BABY

The gun explodes in Martin's mouth.
The boy in the street crap game
looks up with a shocked, broken face.

Dutch:
Shut up you gotta big mouth . . .

233
INTERIOR. STERN'S ROOM. NIGHT. MEDIUM SHOT.

Stern takes another shot. The deck
is almost exhausted. He gets up and
slowly, sadly starts taking the pictures down from the wall.

234
INTERIOR. HOSPITAL ROOM. NIGHT. MEDIUM SHOT.

Dutch's baby hand reaches out and clutches the dollar. His mother is prying it out of his dirty, greasy hand.

Baby Arthur tries to twist away.

Dutch:
Put your greasy mitt in . . . Cut that out we don't owe a nickel . . .

Mrs Flegenheimer:
Stop it, Arthur. Stop it.

Dutch surrenders the dollar.

Dutch:
Sure sure mama.

235
INTERIOR. STERN'S ROOM. NIGHT. MEDIUM SHOT.

The walls are bare. Stern takes his last shot. He takes a piece of dirty, school note paper and writes in pencil:

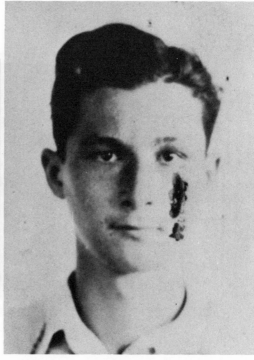

Darling this is good bye. Life is not worth living without you. One who loves you more than life itself. Please take it as I would want you to. Remember the lilacs.

Al

Cut shows newspaper picture of Stern's corpse.

"GANG 'KILLER' IS SUICIDE IN RAGS"

Above Stern's picture is the caption:

"'KILLER' STERN TURNS ON HIMSELF"

HISS OF ESCAPING GAS

HOSPITAL SOUND EFFECTS

236

INTERIOR. HOSPITAL ROOM. NIGHT. MEDIUM SHOT.

Frances Schultz bends over Dutch's bed.

Dutch:
All right, dear, you have to get it now.

Dutch and Frances in pajamas. Dutch gets a cardboard box from a closet.

A million dollars, Frances.

He empties the money onto the bed. Frances rolls around in it like a cat in catnip moaning and giggling as Dutch tears her pajamas off. Sex scene on bed covered with money. Cut back to Dutch on hospital bed. He stirs and moans. Detective puts his hand on Frances Schultz's shoulder.

Detective:
You're just stirring him up, lady. Will you wait outside please.

Frances goes out crying, but we glimpse a cold calculating expression.

1st Detective (he speaks in a wheedling, familiar, obscene voice):
Come on, Dutch, who shot you?

2nd Detective (he speaks in a bullying, peremptory voice):
Come on Dutch who shot you?

ACTION	SOUND

Dutch:
Come on open the soap duckets.

SOUND OF FRYING FAT

Flash of city after atomic attack . . . rubble, heat waves. Boys rush toward the camera with shards and bars of blistered metal. Faces of hatred, evil, and despair. They are in rags, flesh streaked with coal and metal dust which fills the air . . .

Dutch:
The chimney sweeps take to the sword.

1st Detective:
Control yourself.

2nd Detective:
The doctor wants you to lie quiet.

Porter whistles "Home Sweet Home" down the corridor of the Old Harmony Hotel.

Dutch:
But I am dying.

Color shot of advertisement circa 1910 shows blown up soup tin. Written on it in rainbow letters "RAINBOW JACK'S FRENCH CANADIAN BEAN SOUP." Picture on can shows mountain lake, rainbow. The red-haired boy from sex scene dressed as lumberjack holds up the can with the picture on it.

Dutch:
French Canadian bean soup.

Bare room of Albert Stern. He is lying on bed by the open gas oven.

HISS OF ESCAPING GAS

Dutch:
I want to pay.

Sets from film are repeated on loop: Flegenheimer Saloon and Livery Stable, beer drops, offices, Harlem streets, the Old Harmony Hotel, Public School No. 12. The sets are progressively underexposed, darker and darker.

Let them leave me alone.

Stern's plaintive voice:
Arthur Flegenheimer
ARTHUR FLEGENHEIMER

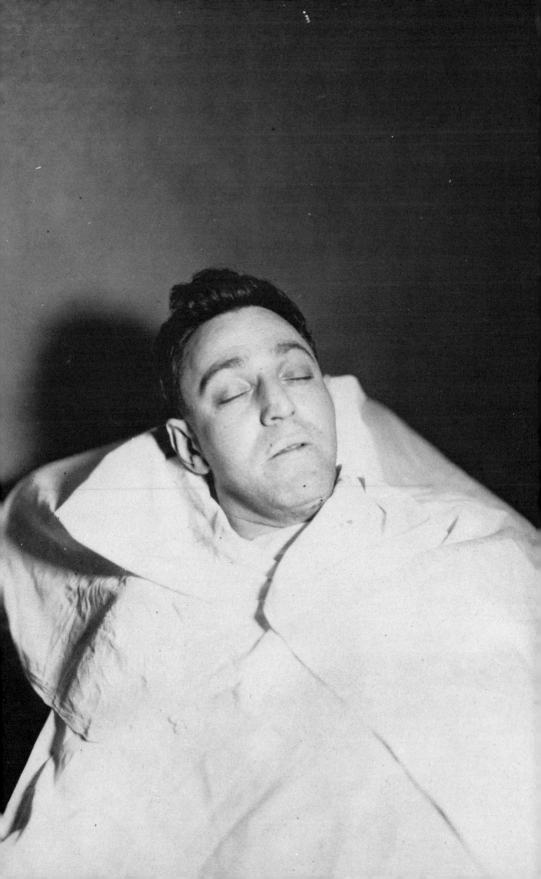

ACTION	SOUND

Mrs Murphy's lilacs flash on screen in bright color.
Sets rapidly darken.

(A last despairing cry)
ARTHUR FLEGENHEIMER

GAS AND HOSPITAL SOUNDS
FAINTER AND FAINTER

Darkness on screen.

SILENCE ON SCREEN

THE END